CEC WAVELENGTHS

**A COURSE IN NARRATIVE COMPREHENSION AND COMPOSITION
FOR CARIBBEAN SECONDARY SCHOOLS**

with stories by

MICHAEL ANTHONY, TIMOTHY CALLENDER,
A. N. FORDE, DENIS FOSTER, BERNARD C. GRAHAM,
CECIL GRAY, MERLE HODGE, C. M. HOPE,
ROBERT A. LUCAS, VIC REID, MONICA SKEETE,
FLORA SQUIRES, ELIZABETH WALCOTT,
JOHN WICKHAM

OXFORD
UNIVERSITY PRESS

OXFORD
UNIVERSITY PRESS

Great Clarendon Street, Oxford, OX2 6DP, United Kingdom

Oxford University Press is a department of the University of Oxford.
It furthers the University's objective of excellence in research, scholarship,
and education by publishing worldwide. Oxford is a registered trade mark of
Oxford University Press in the UK and in certain other countries

First published by Thomas Nelson and Sons Ltd in 1982
This edition published by Oxford University Press in 2014

British Library Cataloguing in Publication Data
Data available

978-0-1756-6318-7

18

Printed by Multivista Global Ltd

CONTENTS

ACKNOWLEDGEMENTS

Cecil Gray and the publishers are very grateful to the following for permission to use the stories which are included in this book. Their cooperation, assistance and enthusiasm have been greatly appreciated.

Michael Anthony for *Enchanted Alley, The Interlude* and *The Valley of Cocoa;* John Wickham for *Alleluia Morning* and *Septimus;* Timothy Callender for *The Sins of the Fathers* and *A Price to Pay;* A. N. Forde for *The Coachman and the Cab* and *Fly Back to Me;* Vic Reid for *No Mourning in the Valley;* Monica Skeete for *The Scholarship;* Flora Spencer for *Aunt Suzie's Rooster;* C. M. Hope for *The Excursion;* Denis Foster for *Banjo;* Elizabeth Walcott for *Pig Money;* Merle Hodge for *Millicent,* and Bernard C. Graham for *When You Were Very Young.*

Thanks are also due to the editors of *Bim* for permission to reprint those stories that first appeared in this literary magazine.

No Mourning in the Valley was first published by Pioneer Press in *Fourteen Jamaican Short Stories.*

The publishers have made every effort to make the list of acknowledgements complete, but in some cases all efforts to trace the owners of copyright failed. It is hoped that any such omissions from the list will be excused.

The author and publishers wish to thank the following for permission to use photographs included in this book:

Craig Burleigh,	page 16
Christopher,	page 45
Camera Press Limited,	page 72
Anne Bolt,	page 94
Verband Deutscher Brieftaubenliebhaber e.V. (Bernd Albrecht)	page 140

Illustrated by Martin Salisbury

TO THE TEACHER

When the anthology *Response* was published in 1969 it was intended for those pupils whose language attainments fitted them for a normal secondary school course at that time, and it seemed to have served its purpose very well. But with the establishment of other types of school, the range of language attainment of the pupils placed in those schools widened to a very considerable degree. That situation called for texts which satisfied very low initial needs while helping the pupils to make progress towards the recognised goals of secondary schooling. A text or texts to replace *Response* was long needed. Yet the popularity of, and demand for *Response* caused the substitution of a different anthology to be postponed until now.

Wavelengths and *Perspectives* are two collections of stories chosen to meet such needs of students in all types of present-day Caribbean secondary shool. Some of the more popular stories previously used in *Response* have been included again, but most of the stories are new and teachers who have used *Response* will recognise that the stories in these two new collections are more aligned to the wider range of language acquisition they now have to deal with, and better graded to allow a steady growth in the pupils' understanding.

Wavelengths is intended for students in either the first or second year of secondary schooling, while *Perspectives* is aimed at students in either the second or third year of the school. But it is the teacher who must make the decision in the light of the previous reading attainments of the student.

In each case the stories have been chosen because they seem to offer enjoyment to the pupils, as that must be the first consideration of the teacher in choosing literary material to present in class. However, to promote any learning at all other objectives must also be set, and the objectives which *Wavelengths* and *Perspectives* can be used to serve are:

1   the development of those comprehension and appreciation skills for enjoying narrative prose fiction;
2   the expansion of the students' passive and active vocabularies in terms of words as well as grammatical structures and sentence patterns;
3   the practice and development of those writing skills for sharing experience in narrative forms;
4   the acquisition of rudimentary insights and concepts needed for appreciation of the short story form.

In both books questions for discussion (*not* testing) are suggested. They are put into two categories and the teacher must decide which ones are useful to his or her pupils in every instance. In the first group are some basic questions to help clarify the story line and to point to relationships to be observed and understood. In the second category are questions to help to develop awareness of the means by which narrative techniques are used in writing stories. Then comes some work to increase the students' word power and give them the means to express their own ideas.

After the necessary discussion to deepen understanding and enjoyment some writing activities are suggested, and attempts are made to link the experience of reading the story to the practice the students need in writing about their own experiences. In this regard teachers are urged to let the students write freely, and not inhibit them with the idea that everything they write is for the teacher to see and mark. There is irrefutable evidence to show the enormous benefits students derive from keeping their own private collections of their own stories, and from putting together class anthologies every six weeks or so. Teachers who have not been exploiting that determinant of interest and motivation are urged to use *Wavelengths* and *Perspectives* for that purpose.

C.G.

1 MILLICENT
Merle Hodge

Tuning in

Everybody remembers something of his or her schooldays, and some writers use their memories to make up stories, as you can do too, if you wish. Merle Hodge, who wrote this story, *Millicent*, is a Trinidadian, and in Trinidad the classes in a primary school are still called *standards*; a little place where cakes, aerated drinks and so on are sold is still sometimes called a *parlour*; and canvas tennis shoes used to be called *crepesoles* or *watchekongs*.

Fourth Standard was a very ordinary class. They came to school for nine o'clock like any other class—or most of them came to school for nine o'clock—for when the bell rang Clem and Harry were usually just pelting across the Savannah. Clem had to tie out his grand-
5 mother's goat before he came to school and Harry had to deliver bottles of milk. They were neighbours, and nearly every morning they dashed into the school yard together and managed to slide in at the back of the line just as Mr Greenidge was closing the gate. Anybody who arrived after the gate was shut had to stand outside and
10 wait until Mr Greenidge was ready to let them in and lead them to the Headmaster's office.

Fourth Standard was very ordinary. They had as many fights as anybody else. They fought over the duster because everybody wanted to clean the blackboard; they fought over who was to be at the head of
15 the line in mornings; they fought in Miss Aggie's parlour at recess time and at lunch time, fought and pushed like anybody else to get their dinner-mints or sweet-biscuits or tamarind-balls. And they didn't fight when it was their turn to clean the latrines; then, they just ran and hid all over the place.
20 There were twenty-two girls and eighteen boys, so the girls always won when the class played cricket or tug-o'-war, girls against boys.

Fourth Standard had its Duncey-Head and its Bright-Spark like any other class. Joel Price couldn't read further than Page Nine. He was stuck at Page Nine for so long that he could say it by heart with his
25 eyes closed, but when Miss turned the page and he saw Page Ten he would hang his head and his eyes filled up with water. And Emily Joseph was so bright that everybody said that her mother gave her bulb porridge in the morning and bulb soup in the night.

Miss was nice sometimes. She didn't beat as much as Mr Gomes or
30 Mrs Davies, and she didn't beat for silly little things like forgetting

1

your pen at home or getting all your sums wrong.

But she got very angry if somebody talked while she was talking. Sandra and Shira were always getting into trouble because they chatted and chatted like a pair of parrots all day long. Miss promised
35 them that when we went on the zoo outing she was going to put them in the big cage with the parrots and leave them there. Miss said the parrots at the zoo had a nice big roomy cage big enough for two talkative young ladies to take up residence, and the parrots would be glad of their company.

40 Other things she would beat for were not doing your homework, and stealing. When something was stolen, nobody knew how she found out who the thief was, but Miss was always right. As soon as she learned that there had been a theft, she tapped the ruler on the table to call the class to attention. Then she stood and stared at us; she
45 looked at our faces one by one, very slowly, and when she had looked at everybody in turn she started again from the front row, while everybody sat and held their breath; and then her eyes stopped at one face and everybody breathed again and all turned to see who the 'culprit was. In Fourth Standard you couldn't get away with stealing.

50 Miss was nice because she took her class outside more often than anybody else. The other children all envied Fourth Standard because whenever the afternoon got really hot we would be seen filing out towards the Savannah. Anybody who talked or made any noise on the way out would be sent back to sit with his book in the empty
55 classroom, but of course nobody was willing to run this risk, so we filed out silently and in the most orderly manner.

Miss said that Fourth Standard was the worst class in the school, but we knew that she'd said the same thing to every Fourth Standard class she'd had, so we didn't believe her. For, all things considered, Fourth
60 Standard was no better or no worse than any other class; they were a very ordinary class.

And then Millicent came. Millicent came and brought pure ruction.

One Monday morning there she was, sitting in the third row in a bright red organdy dress and red ribbons and smelling of baby
65 powder. She was sharing a desk with Parbatee and Eric and Vena and Harry. The desk was only made for four, but Miss put her there because Parbatee and Eric and Vena and Harry were all very small and didn't quite fill up the bench. But there was Millicent sitting in the middle, with her elbows sprawled on the desk either side of her, and
70 her skirt spread out on the bench, so that Parbatee and Eric were squeezed together at one end of the bench, and Vena and Harry looked as though they were about to fall off the other end. Millicent sat like a queen in the middle.

The other four sat cramped for the whole morning, barely able to
75 write, but not daring to complain for Millicent and her red organdy

2

dress filled them with awe.

But by mid-afternoon Millicent had taken over so much of the bench that Harry really fell off his end. All we heard was a little crash, because Harry was not very big (in fact, we called him 'Mosquito').
80 We heard a crash and a small shriek and Harry was sitting in the aisle ready to burst with anger.

Everybody laughed, the class was in uproar. Miss was laughing helplessly too, but then she made her face stern again and tapped the ruler on the table. Harry picked himself up and stayed standing in the
85 aisle, looking at Millicent in such a way that if looks could kill Millicent would have dropped down dead in her red organdy dress.

'Millicent, you will sit at the end,' said Miss.

'NOPE!' said Millicent and she folded her arms, pouted her mouth and stayed where she was.
90 Everybody was shocked. This girl must be crazy! We stopped all our laughter and stared in amazement. Even Harry forgot to be angry and stared dumbfounded at Millicent, then at Miss, from one to the other.

There was complete silence. We were a little excited, waiting to see
95 what would happen next, looking at Miss's face.

'Come out here, Ma'am,' said Miss.

Millicent still sat with her arms tightly folded and her mouth pushed far out like a pig-snout. Then Miss started to get up, her chair grated on the floor. Our hearts beat faster. This crazy girl didn't know our
100 Miss—she wasn't afraid of her in her organdy dress, she would put the ruler on her, organdy dress or no organdy dress.

But when Millicent saw that Miss was going to come for her, she suddenly sprang up and pushed Vena off the bench to get out. Vena didn't fall right down, but she hit her elbow on the edge of the desk,
105 and that made her so angry that she flew at Millicent and landed her a cuff right in the middle of her chest. Miss rushed down the aisle and parted them.

Millicent was crying loudly, saying she was going to tell her Auntie June, and she didn't like this old dirty country-school, and her father
110 was going to come and take her back to Belmont . . .

Miss clapped her hands sharply:

'Get your spelling books, everybody outside, no noise; and you Ma'am, if you make one more sound, you will sit down right here by yourself.'
115 The rest of us were nearly outside already, Millicent stood sniffling still, rather bewildered at the sight of the classroom emptying around her. Then she wiped her nose and followed.

Out on the Savannah we quickly settled down, some sitting on the grass, some on the old tree trunk. Joel brought the chair for Miss.
120 Millicent stood apart and looked on scornfully. We soon forgot

about her, because there was a nice breeze blowing, and Miss asked us easy words—even Joel was able to spell two whole words, so he was wearing a broad smile. Everybody forgot about Millicent. We didn't even know she had walked off.

125 And then suddenly the ground seemed to shake and we heard something like thunder mixed with screaming, and we looked and saw this red shape flying across the Savannah towards us. In one second there was a stampede. We had tumbled off the tree trunk, those on the grass had scrambled to their feet, spelling books were lying 130 scattered on the ground and the whole of Fourth Standard was running, pelting towards the school, everybody screaming with all their might.

Mr Jeremy's bull was loose! And nobody know how Millicent had managed to offend Mr Jeremy's bull, but it was chasing her furiously, 135 pounding after her, snorting and cursing her in cow language, and she was tearing across the grass, her red organdy dress flying in the breeze.

Nobody looked back until we were inside the schoolyard. Then we looked out and saw Miss bringing Millicent who was crying bitterly, holding one of her ribbons in her hand, the sashes of her dress hanging 140 down.

The next morning Millicent appeared in a bright yellow organdy dress and yellow ribbons. She sat at the end but placed her big plaid bag on the bench beside her because, she said, she didn't want either Picky-Head Congo Vena or Roti-Coolie Harry near her. Vena went 145 and complained to Miss.

Again we held our breaths. Once, we had just come up to Fourth Standard, she shared licks for half an hour one afternoon when she got the news that at lunchtime a little fight between Carl and Deo had grown into a war with nearly the whole of Fourth Standard divided 150 into two gangs calling each other Coolie and Nigger. She told us that everybody's great-grandfather was both a Coolie and a Nigger—Deodath's great-grandfather was a Nigger and Carl's great-grandfather was a Coolie, because Coolie and Nigger just meant beast of burden, and that all our great-grandparents were made to be, but if 155 that was what we wanted to be then she would lick us like beasts of burden; she sent a boy to borrow Mr Gomes' strap, went on the rampage and shared out some unforgettable licks. That was the last of that.

When Vena went and complained to Miss she shot up and strode 160 down the aisle to Millicent.

'Pack up your bag, Ma'am,' she said.

Millicent held on to her bag and Miss yanked her out of the seat and marched her to the back of the class. She told the children in one of the back rows to take their desk to the front, while she sent some others to 165 get one of the old desks from downstairs.

4

This ruction lasted for about fifteen minutes and we enjoyed it thoroughly. At the end of it all, the back row children were installed in front, and in the back row, in an old rickety desk for four sat Millicent and her plaid bag. Millicent in her yellow organdy dress. She was not
170 very pleased.

At recess time she picked up her bag and walked solemnly to Miss Aggie's parlour (everybody else *ran* to be there first). When she got there she didn't join the pushing and jostling, she just stood, looking so angelic in her yellow organdy dress and yellow ribbons that Miss
175 Aggie was impressed, stopped serving us and called out to her:

'What you want, little girl?'

Millicent smiled sweetly, took one step forward and the whole unruly crowd of us fell silent and automatically parted in two, making way for her.

180 She walked to the counter and put down a dollar bill. A whole dollar bill! Our eyes nearly fell out of our heads, and a low sound of 'Ooooooo!' rose from the crowd.

'Ten cents' dinner-mints please, and ten cents' paradise plums, and six cents' saltprunes, and . . .' Miss Aggie moved from bottle to
185 bottle, her eyes widening all the time.

Millicent spent the whole dollar. She stuffed all that she had bought into the bag and turned to go. We were following her every movement. She walked out of the parlour without looking right or left.

By afternoon recess Millicent sat on a bench in the yard surrounded
190 by a court of seven. These were the Chosen Few: Clem, Diane, Shira, Joel, Anthony, Fazeeda and Gayle. Their mouths were full, and as they chewed away their eyes were fixed admiringly upon Millicent.

The next morning Millicent arrived in a pink dress, and Miss asked her when she was going to get her uniform. She said her Auntie June
195 hadn't got it yet.

At recess time as she sat holding court, she was heard to say loudly to her group of admirers:

'She think I don't have my uniform hanging up in my press? What I must wear uniform for? I not wearing any uniform. I have a whole
200 press full of clothes and shoes and toys . . .'

The news reached Miss, and that afternoon Millicent went home with a letter from Miss to her Auntie June. The next morning Millicent came to school wearing blue overall, white blouse and a scowl on her face. She was very sour indeed.

205 That morning Clem came to school without Harry. Millicent had told him to have nothing to do with Harry or she wouldn't talk to him any more.

At lunchtime we started up a game of cricket. Faraz and Anthony were the best batters, and Gayle could bowl down wickets like peas,
210 so everybody wanted them on their side. Somebody went to look for

5

Gayle and Anthony. They were in the parlour with Millicent and they didn't feel like playing cricket. So the rest of us played a stupid dull game.

When Sandra came back from lunch she went in search of Shira, for she had so much to tell her and they hadn't had a chance to talk in class all morning, because Miss had kept her eye on the two of them. She didn't get to talk to Shira at morning recess either, because she spent the whole of recess in the latrine. Her mother had given them salts the day before, and that was one of the things she had to tell Shira about, how her mother and her grandmother had to run after the six of them, round and round the house until they caught them one by one and held their noses and made them drink the salts. She was dying to get into a cosy conversation with Shira.

She looked around the Savannah for her and didn't find her. Then she went into the schoolyard, walked around, and spotted her on the tank with some others playing jacks. She ran happily towards her, calling out her name:

'Shira! Shira!!'

Shira turned around to see who it was and then coldly turned her back. Sandra thought she hadn't seen her and went right up to the tank and touched Shira on her shoulder.

Shira brushed her off: 'Leave me in peace, nuh!'

Sandra was flabbergasted and didn't move. Millicent drew herself up:

'You wash your foot before you come in the dance? Shoo! We don't want any picky-head tar-babies here.' And the rest of the gang giggled.

Sandra ran away and hid in a corner until the bell rang.

By the end of the week Millicent's gang had grown to fifteen. They stopped playing on the Savannah. Millicent brought a fancy skipping-rope, jacks, ludo, dominoes and pretty story books. With these, as well as all the sweets she bought, she held them captive at recess and at lunchtime.

She got them to run to the parlour for her, do her homework for her, fetch water for her in her pretty Mickey-Mouse cup . . .

The rest of us didn't know what to do. Nobody any longer thought of going and telling Miss on her. For there were a lot of us who would give anything to join Millicent's gang and didn't want to offend her. And even those who hated her were afraid of her.

Fourth Standard became a sour, quarrelsome class. Millicent's gang didn't have much to do with the rest of us, and the rest of us had more fights among ourselves than ever before. We began to call each other 'Cassava Nigger' and 'Polorie Coolie,' terms we had learnt from Millicent. Almost every time we started a game it ended in a fight. Somebody always said the score-keeper was cheating or the bowler

6

was aiming the ball at the batsman's belly for spite.

And Millicent reigned supreme. She managed not to get any licks because her homework was always done, and she couldn't get into trouble for talking in class when there was nobody sitting with her. And she didn't get any licks at home either. Everybody knew that her Auntie June let her stay up until any hour she wanted, even midnight; that she never had to wash dishes or sweep; that when she got home from school she just sprawled off in an armchair and her Autie June took off her shoes and socks for her and immediately brought her ice-cream and cake; that her mother, who was in America, sent her a box full of clothes and shoes and toys every week . . . Millicent was a heroine out of a story-book.

We no longer considered her to be sitting in disgrace at the back of the class in the desk all by herself. She was a princess sitting on a throne, and nobody was really good enough to sit on the same bench as Millicent.

Of course Miss knew that all was not well in the class. She called Harry and asked him why he and Clem didn't come to school together any more. Harry's eyes filled up with water and he wouldn't say a word. She called Clem and asked him. Clem wriggled uncomfortably and said his grandmother made him get up earlier to go and tie out the goat, and he couldn't wait for Harry again. Tears started to run down Harry's cheeks. Everybody felt ashamed but nobody would say a word, for Millicent was sitting surveying us all from her throne at the back of the class.

Miss sent Harry and Clem back to their seats.

'So nobody in this class has anything to tell me this week,' she said, 'not even the news-carriers. Hm.'

We sat and squirmed. Miss looked at everybody then she looked straight over our heads to the back of the class and said, slowly and terribly:

'Pride goeth before a fall.'

Nobody had the faintest idea what this meant, but we knew it meant something very grim and unpleasant. Everybody knew that she had looked at Millicent as she said it, but no one dared even glance back at Millicent. Nobody would risk offending Millicent.

Matters grew worse over the next few weeks. Millicent threw Joel out of her gang. She had sent him to the parlour with ten cents to buy three cents' dinner-mints, five tamarind balls and a packet of chewing gum, and he came back with twenty dinner-mints. She told him he was so stupid he had no right to live. Joel cried for two days.

We all knew that Millicent would now be looking around for a new member to replace Joel, so we were extra courteous to her for the next few days. We remarked to each other how nice Millicent's hair-style was, how clean her crepesoles, how enviable her complexion: we

vowed within her hearing that we couldn't stand blackie Picky-Head
Niggers and greasy Roti-Coolies. We declared that we found Miss to
be an out-of-place frowsy old hog, always trying to boss people
about. We smiled nervously at Millicent, who ignored us completely.
305   And soon Millicent's verdict was made known: the new member
was Christine Reece. The rest of us were heartbroken. We now hated
Christine Reece with all our might, but continued to do everything we
could to get into Millicent's good books.

Nobody bothered to start any games on the Savannah any more.
310 We hung about the schoolyard and sulked, casting envious sidelong
glances at Millicent and her gang. And Millicent continued to look
upon us with scorn.

Then it was the end of term test. Millicent announced that she was
coming first, that Emily Joseph didn't know as much as she knew
315 because she didn't have all the books that she had, and Emily's mother
couldn't buy Brain Food for her like her mother sent from America.

And there was no question in anybody's mind—of course Millicent
was going to come first. She was the prettiest, richest, luckiest,
bravest, quickest, funniest, cleanest, healthiest child in the class, so
320 naturally she was also the brightest; she didn't even have to say so, for
everybody knew. Even Emily Joseph knew. Emily Joseph wouldn't
dare come higher than Millicent.

Miss gave the arithmetic test first. Millicent finished long before
everybody else and closed her copy-book, while Emily Joseph was
325 still writing and counting on her fingers. When we came out Millicent
boasted to her gang that she had got out all the sums in two two's.

In the afternoon we had dictation. Millicent wrote rapidly, never
stopping to look at Miss.

The end-of-term test lasted for two days, and the next day at
330 lunchtime Millicent gave a 'party' for her gang to celebrate her success
in the exam. She had brought apples from home, and pretty paper
cups with Mickey Mouse on them. She sent messengers to Miss
Aggie's parlour to buy soft drinks and sweet biscuits. They had a feast,
and we hung a little distance away pretending not to notice them; but
335 if Millicent had thrown an apple stem to us we would have fought
over it like dogs.

The bell rang and we went in. Millicent's gang rubbing their bellies
and making sounds of satisfaction, Millicent sailing in with her head in
the air.
340   When we had settled down, Miss said, 'Test results,' and everybody
shouted 'Raaaaaay!' including Joel who was never anywhere but last.

'Where to begin?' Miss asked, 'top or bottom?'

There was commotion for a while, some shouting 'Top! Top!!'
some shouting 'Bottom! Bottom!!' and some even shouting 'Middle!'
345   Then we realised that Millicent's gang was shouting 'Top! Top!!' so

8

everybody shouted with them. Of course if Miss started from the bottom of the list Millicent would have to wait for forty-one names before she heard hers, which was, of course, at the top.

'Okay, okay, I'll start from the top. Quiet, or I won't read them at all.'

She picked up the list, put on her glasses, and everybody looked at Millicent with admiration and then turned to look at Miss again.

'First—Emily Joseph.'

We jumped. Emily looked frightened. Nobody dared look back at Millicent. Miss was reading on; Fifth, sixth, seventh . . . We were worried. She must have forgotten Millicent! Eleventh, twelfth, thirteenth . . . Decidedly something was wrong.

By the time Miss had got to thirtieth we were paralysed. Nobody could move. We held our breaths. Thirty-second, thirty-third . . . You could have heard a pin drop. We wanted to stop Miss, to make her start over again, because she had skipped over Millicent's name.

'Thirty-ninth—Faraz Mohammed. Fortieth—Joel Price. Forty-first—Millicent Hernandez.

Several seconds passed before we could breathe again.

Then we heard a giggle, and we couldn't believe it had come from our class. But it had, Vena had her hand over her mouth and was shaking with laughter. She looked at Harry. A smile spread over Harry's face. He put his head down on the desk and giggled. Snickers came from different parts of the class. Miss was calmly putting away her list.

The giggles and snickers grew. Soon the whole class was laughing as loudly as we had laughed the day Harry fell off the bench. Miss turned her back and cleaned the blackboard.

When she had finished cleaning the blackboard she gave us the ball and sent out outside because, she said, we were the most unruly class in the whole school, and in the whole of Trinidad and Tobago.

We poured out onto the Savannah.

'Football!' somebody shouted.

'Girls against boys!' said another.

'Not fair!' said a boy's voice, 'its 23 girls against 18 boys.'

'Which twenty-three?' asked somebody, 'it's only twenty-two girls. Let's go!'

It was the best football game we ever had. Nobody won because there was so much laughing and rolling about that we forgot to keep the score. The goal-post kept falling down and Joel wet his pants.

Somebody shouted: 'Mr Jeremy bull!' and we scattered, screaming, in all directions; and when we realised there was no bull we lay down on the grass and laughed till we were weak.

Then we tried to start the game again, but Clem grabbed the ball and ran off with it, and everybody ran after him, so he threw it to another boy and soon the game turned into Sway, and when it was Sway the boys always managed to keep the ball, the girls never got hold of it . . .

And it was only twenty-two girls, because Millicent was sitting in
395 the schoolyard, all by herself.

Talking about it

A *The events of the story*

1 Why did the storyteller think Fourth Standard was an ordinary class?
2 Who was Miss, and what are you told about her?
3 When did the fight between Carl and Deo take place?
4 Which friendships did Millicent cause to break up, and how?
5 What big change took place in Fourth Standard because of Millicent?
6 Why did everybody think they knew how Millicent was treated at home?
7 What things did Millicent do to get the boys and girls in the class to give her special treatment?
8 What did the test results cause to happen?

B *The writing skills*

1 A story is called a *narrative*, and the person who is telling the story in the story is called a *narrator*. Sometimes the author takes the part of the narrator and tells the story from that *point of view*, using words like *we, us, our, I*, and so on. Who is the narrator in *Millicent*, and from whose *point of view* is the story told?
2 What two reasons did the narrator have for saying Miss was nice?
3 What joke is made about electric light bulbs?
4 What fault in Millicent do you think really made the class turn against her?
5 Whatever we make up out of our imaginations is called *fiction* and if it is a story it is called *prose fiction* or *narrative fiction*. Most people make up a story by first making up or imagining or remembering a person or persons. Those made-up or imaginary persons are called *characters* (say 'K Aracters') in a story or a play. Who would you say is the main character in *Millicent*, and why?
6 The way a writer uses language in telling a story, or the kind of language the writer uses, is called the *style* of the story. In *Millicent* the author uses words and phrases like *nice, best, pure ruction, duncey-head, shared licks, batters, like peas*, and so on. What do you think of the *style* she used?

7   A story tells that certain things happened to a person or persons, or that a person or persons did certain things. So you might be tempted to say a story is just about a person or persons. But, in truth, a story is usually about more than just a particular person or persons. It is usually really about something that people can notice generally about everyday life, like how quarrels grow, or how children learn their parents' feelings, or what fear can do to a child, or something like that. That is called the *theme* of the story; it is what the story is really about, apart from the particular characters in it. Which of these do you think best describes the *theme* of Millicent?

   a) how strange things happen
   b) the dullness of life in school
   c) pride goes before a fall
   d) how teachers make mistakes

C   *The use of words*

1   Here are some words used in the story, *Millicent*. Look back at how each one is used and make a thoughtful guess about its meaning.

   culprit (1.49)   *shriek* (1.80)   *pouted* (1.88)   *amazement* (1.91)
   bewildered (1.116)   *stampede* (1.128)   *furiously* (1.134)
   rampage (1.157)   *ruction* (1.166)

   Now discuss which one of them best fits into each blank space in this paragraph.
   There was a dead rat on my desk. The _____ that I let out caused the class to _____ through the door as if they were going on a _____. The teacher was _____ by their behaviour and looked at them in _____ as they rushed out. Then she strode _____ to the door as we heard the _____ they were making outside. She turned to me and asked if I knew who the _____ was who put the dead rat on my desk, but I only stood there and _____ in shame and embarrassment.

2   The words in italics are used in the story, *Millicent*. Look back at how each one is used, make a thoughtful guess about its meaning, and then discuss which one of the other words in the same row is nearest in meaning to it.

   residence (1.38)   home   occupants   district   employment
   aisle (1.80)   floor   lane   avenue   mountain
   scowl (1.204)   cry   mask   grin   frown
   flabbergasted (1.233)   beaten   amazed   flattened   bored

11

wriggled (l.275)	built	danced	twisted	ran
courteous (l.298)	polite	proud	painful	snobbish
enviable (l.300)	envious	admirable	hostile	permissible

Beaming out

Doing your own thing

First you must make or get yourself a folder of some kind to keep your work in. Put a title on it like *My Own Stories* or *First Steps in Fiction* or *Stories By An Ordinary Person* or *Creative Efforts* or something like that. In that folder you will be keeping stories and descriptions that you will write this year.

When you are writing a story remember you are doing it for whoever you wish to show it to. You are not writing it for the teacher unless you wish to show it to him or her. The teacher cannot read and 'mark' everything that everybody in the class writes—unless the teacher allows you to write now and then only when you should be writing all the time, and so denies you the chance to get the amount of practice that you need if you are to improve.

From time to time you may show the teacher something from your folder and ask for his or her opinion. But most of the time you will be sharing your efforts with your friends and giving them your opinions about theirs.

When everybody in the class has at least one good story in his or her folder, choose someone to collect one story from each person in the class—the story that that person wants to be put in the collection. Each story must carry the author's name. Then they should be tied or sewn together with an attractive cover having a title on it like *Best Stories of New Writers* or *Best of This Term* or *Personal Choice* or whatever you wish, and the collection or anthology should be placed in the school library for the whole school to read.

You should be able to produce such a collection or anthology once or twice a term.

Now, to begin, this week in your spare time try to do one of these, or any other story you wish, and put it in your folder.

1 Imagine you are Millicent. That is, imagine you see things from Millicent's point of view, especially from the time the test results were read out to the time when the whole class left you by yourself.

 Write an account of what happened then, as Millicent would have told it to somebody outside the school.

2 Think back to a primary school class you were in and try to remember as much as you can about some of the other boys and

girls who were in it too. Then try to see if you can recall an incident that took place, in the class or outside, with some members of the class being involved in it.

When you remember enough about the occasion, write an account of it in the same way as Merle Hodge wrote *Millicent*. Put it in your folder to show your friends.

3   Think about a teacher you had two or three years ago, but give him or her a different name and change some other things about him or her, like age, build, complexion, and so on. Then make up some other things about him or her, like what he or she wanted very much in life, what was preventing him or her getting that wish, and so on.

By that time you will be almost ready to picture a story in your imagination about the character you have made up. So try to imagine it—where it took place, when, why, who else was involved, how, what happened, and so on. When you have a kind of outline in your head think of how you could begin the story—not by describing the person—in a very interesting way, and begin to write it.

Continue writing it whenever you get a little spare time, and when it is finished give it a title and your name, and put it for safe keeping in your folder.

2 ENCHANTED ALLEY
Michael Anthony

Tuning in

Many of us see certain places and people every day and yet if someone asks us to tell about those places and people we think there is nothing we can say, or that what we can say is not interesting. But Michael Anthony did not think so, and, although the people he tells us about in this story do not dress or speak like that nowadays, he makes us experience being there at that time with him. If you wish to learn to write stories you can do no better than to begin by imitating Michael Anthony.

(An *alley* is a narrow lane; *enchanted* means charmed or delighted; a *loin-cloth* is a length of cloth worn by a man wrapped around his hips and between his legs; a *saree* (or *sari*) is a length of cloth wrapped around a woman as a dress.)

Leaving for school early on mornings I walked slowly through the busy parts of the town. The business places would all be opening then and smells of strange fragrance would fill the High Street. Inside the opening doors I would see clerks dusting, arranging, hanging
5 things up, getting ready for the day's business. They looked cheerful and eager and they opened the doors very wide. Sometimes I stood up to watch them.

In places between the stores several little alleys ran off the High Street. Some were busy and some were not, and there was one that
10 was long and narrow and dark and very strange. Here too the shops would be opening as I passed and there would be bearded Indians in loin-cloths spreading rugs on the pavement. There would be Indian women also, with veils thrown over their shoulders, setting up their stalls and chatting in a strange sweet tongue. Often I stood, too,
15 watching them, and taking in the fragrance of rugs and spices and onions and sweetmeats. And sometimes, suddenly remembering, I would hurry away for fear the school bell had gone.

In class, long after I settled down, the thoughts of this alley would return to me. I recalled certain stalls and certain beards and certain
20 flashing eyes, and even some of the rugs that had been rolled out. The Indian women, too, with bracelets around their ankles and around their sun-browned arms flashed to my mind. I thought of them. I saw them again looking slyly at me from under the shadow of the stores, their veils half-hiding their faces. In my mind I could almost picture
25 them laughing together and talking in that strange sweet tongue. And

14

mostly the day would be quite old before the spell of the alley wore off my mind.

One morning I was much too early for school. I passed street sweepers at work on the Promenade and when I came to the High Street only one or two shop doors were open. I walked slowly, absorbing the quietness and noticing some of the alleys that ran away to the backs of fences and walls and distant streets. I looked at the names of these alleys. Some were very funny. And I walked on anxiously so I could look a little longer at the dark funny street.

As I walked it struck me that I did not know the name of that street. I laughed at myself. Always I had stood there looking along it and I did not know the name of it. As I drew near I kept my eyes on the wall of the corner shop. There was no sign on the wall. On getting there I looked at the other wall. There was a sign-plate upon it but the dust had gathered thick there and whatever the sign said was hidden behind the dust.

I was disappointed. I looked along the alley which was only now beginning to get alive, and as the shop doors opened the enchantment of spice and onions and sweetmeats emerged. I looked at the wall again but there was nothing there to say what the street was called. Straining my eyes at the signplate I could make out a C and an A, but farther along the dust had made one smooth surface of the plate and the wall.

'Stupes!' I said in disgust. I heard mild laughter, and as I looked before me I saw the man rolling out his rugs. There were two women beside him and they were talking together and they were laughing and I could see the women were pretending not to look at me. They were setting up a stall of sweetmeats and the man put down his rugs and took out something from a tray and put it into his mouth, looking back at me. Then they talked again in the strange tongue and laughed.

I stood there a while. I knew they were talking about me. I was not afraid. I wanted to show them that I was not timid and that I wouldn't run away. I moved a step or two nearer the wall. The smell rose up stronger now and they seemed to give the feelings of things splendoured and far away. I pretended I was looking at the wall but I stole glances at the merchants from the corner of my eyes. I watched the men in their loin-cloths and the garments of the women were full and many coloured and very exciting. The women stole glances at me and smiled to each other and ate of the sweetmeats they sold. The rug merchant spread out his rugs wide on the pavement and he looked at the beauty of their colours and seemed very proud. He too looked slyly at me.

I drew a little nearer because I was not timid of them. There were many more stalls now under the stores. Some of the people turned off the High Street and came into this little alley and they bought little

things of the merchants. The merchants held up the bales of cloth and matched them on to the people's clothes, and I could see they were saying it was very nice. I smiled at this, and the man with the rugs saw me and smiled.

5   That made me brace. I thought of the word I knew in the strange tongue and when I remembered it I drew nearer.

'Salaam,' I said.

The rug merchant laughed aloud and the two women laughed aloud and I laughed too. Then the merchant bowed low to me and replied,

0 'Salaam!'

This was very amusing for the two women. They talked together so I couldn't understand and then the fat one spoke.

'Wot wrang wid de warl?'

I was puzzled for a moment and then I said, 'O, is the street sign.

5 Dust cover it.'

'Street sign?' one said, and they covered their laughter with their veils.

'I can't read what street it is,' I said. 'What street this is?'

The rug merchant spoke to the two women in the strange tongue

0 and the three of them giggled and one of the women said: 'Every marning you stand up dey and you don' know what they carl here?'

'First time I come down here,' I said.

'Yes,' said the fat woman. Her face was big and friendly and she sat squat on the pavement. 'First time you wark down here but every

5 marning you stop dey and watch we.'

I laughed.

'You see 'e laughing?' said the other. The rug merchant did not say anything but he was very much amused.

'What you call this street?' I said. I felt very brave because I knew

00 they were friendly to me, and I looked at the stalls, and the smell of the sweetmeats was delicious. There was *barah* too, and chutney and dry *channa*, and in a square tin there was the wet yellow *channa*, still hot, the steam curling up from it.

The man took time to put down his rugs and then he spoke to me.

05 'This,' he said, talking slowly and making actions with his arms, 'from up dey to up dey is Calcutta Street.' He was very pleased with his explanation. He had pointed from the High Street end of the alley to the other end that ran darkly into the distance. The whole street was very long and dusty, and in the concrete drain there was no water and

110 the brown peel of onions blew about when there was a little wind. Sometimes there was the smell of cloves in the air and sometimes the smell of oil-cloths, but where I stood the smell of the sweetmeats was strongest and most delicious.

'You like Calcutta Street?'

115 'Yes,' I said.

The two women laughed coyly and looked from one to the other.

'I have to go,' I said, '—school.'

'O you gwine to school?' the man said. He put down his rugs again. His loin-cloth was very tight around him. 'Well, you could wark so,' he said, pointing away from the High Street end of the alley, 'and when you get up dey, turn so, and when you wark and wark, you'll meet school.'

'Oh,' I said, surprised. I didn't know there was a way to school along this alley.

'You see?' he said, very pleased with himself.

'Yes,' I said.

The two women looked at him smiling and they seemed very proud the way he explained. I moved off to go, holding my books under my arm. The women looked at me and they smiled in a sad, friendly way. I looked at the chutney and *barah* and *channa* and suddenly something occurred to me. I felt in my pockets and then I opened my books and looked among the pages. I heard one of the women whisper—'Taking larning . . . ' 'Aha . . . ' said the other and I did not hear the rest of what she said. Desperately I turned the books down and shook them and the penny fell out rolling on the pavement. I grabbed it up and turned to the fat woman. For a moment I couldn't decide which, but the delicious smell of the yellow wet *channa* softened my heart.

'A penny *channa*,' I said. 'Wet.'

The woman bent over the big spoon, took out a small paper-bag, flapped it open, then crammed two or three spoonfuls of *channa* into it. Then she took up the pepper bottle.

'Pepper?'

'Yes,' I said, anxiously.

'Plenty?'

'Plenty.'

The fat woman laughed, pouring the pepper sauce with two or three pieces of red pepper-skin falling on the *channa*.

'Food!' I said, licking my lips.

'You see?' said the other woman; she grinned widely, her gold teeth glittering in her mouth. 'You see 'e like plenty pepper?'

As I handed my penny I saw the long brown fingers of the rug merchant stretching over my head. He handed a penny to the fat lady.

'You keep you penny in your pocket,' he grinned at me, 'an look out, you go reach to school late.'

I was very grateful about the penny. I slipped it into my pocket.

'You could wark so,' the man said, pointing up Calcutta Street, 'an' turn so, and you'll come down by the school.'

'Yes,' I said, hurrying off.

The street was alive with people now. There were many more merchants with rugs and many more stalls of sweetmeats and other

things. I saw bales of bright cloth matched up to ladies' dresses and I heard the ladies laugh and say it was good. I walked fast through the crowd. There were women with sarees calling out 'Ground-nuts! *Parata!*' and every here and there gramophones blared out Indian
165 songs. I walked on with my heart full inside me. Sometimes I stood up to listen and then I walked on again. Then suddenly it came home to me it must be very late. The crowd was thick and the din spread right along Calcutta Street. I looked back to wave to my friends. They were far behind and the pavement was so crowded I could not see. I heard
170 the car horns tooting and I knew that on the High Street it must be a jam-session of traffic and people. It must be very late. I held my books in my hands, secured the paper-bag of *channa* in my pocket, and with the warmth against my legs I ran pell-mell to school.

Talking about it

A *The events of the story*

1 Whom did the narrator sometimes stand to watch on his way to school?
2 What thoughts usually remained with him in class long after he had settled down?
3 Why did he have a chance to linger longer the morning of the story?
4 Why did he say *Stupes* in disgust?
5 What did he do when he pretended to be looking at the wall?
6 How did he greet the merchant and women?
7 *I was puzzled for a moment* (1.84). Why do you think he was puzzled?
8 Why do you suppose the woman laughed when he said *street sign* (1.84)?
9 What had the fat woman seen him do before?
10 What smelled delicious to him?
11 What was the man *very pleased with himself* about (1.106)?
12 *Suddenly it came home to me* (1.166). What occurred to him?
13 What did the woman mean by *Takin larning* (1.132)?
14 Who paid the fat woman for the channa the narrator asked for?
15 *The street was alive with people now* (1.159). What things were they doing?

B *The writing skills*

1 Notice what the writer's sentences are like in the story—his *style*. Would you say the style is

    a   simple, unpretentious and honest;
    b   complicated, high-falutin', and formal;
    c   unusual, dense, and show-off?

2 Why do you suppose the writer put in so many little details of what the narrator saw, heard, smelled and felt?

3 Why did the writer have the sellers speak in such a way, saying things like *Wot wrang wid de warl* (1.83), and so on?

4 What would you say the writer did to get readers to understand what he thought and how he felt?

5 The writer uses *I* in telling the story. So the story is told from inside the narrator, i.e. from the narrator's *point of view*. Do you think that makes you feel more inside the story yourself, or would it have been better if the writer had used *he*—telling the story from the point of view of someone outside the story?

C *The use of words*

To learn how to use words of a language you must notice how persons who know the language well use the words. Then you must try to use them yourself in speaking and writing.

1 Look back and notice where and how each of these words is used in the story—the context of the word—and figure out what it might mean, if you did not know before.

fragrance (1.3)   *eager* (1.6)   *disgust* (1.49)   *occurred* (1.131)
desperately (1.134)   *anxiously* (1.143)   *glittering* (1.150)   *din* (1.167)

2 Now fit each of the words above into one of these sentences:

    a)   The pieces of broken glass _____ in the sun.
    b)   A strange thing _____ yesterday morning.
    c)   I like to breathe in the _____ of the flowers.
    d)   We were very _____ to help in the cleaning up.
    e)   He was waiting _____ to see what she would do to him.
    f)   The loud _____ of the traffic kept me from sleeping.
    g)   I was full of _____ with myself for forgetting my ticket.
    h)   They were _____ trying to prevent the fire from spreading.

3 Now try to use those words in oral sentences of your own.

4 What is the missing letter in each of these words?
    abs★rbing   s★rface   mil★   splendo★r
    sq★at   delic★ous   gr★teful   sec★red

Beaming out

The story, *Enchanted Alley*, is an excellent example of what you can do and must do. Michael Anthony is one of the best writers of the Caribbean. His style is simple, unpretentious and honest, although his themes are usually deep. He deals with the things that people really live through, and he makes us see how important they are.

For your folder you could work on one of these this week. Do it in your spare time and keep it for your friends and your teacher to enjoy and discuss with you if you wish. Later on you might want to put it into your class anthology.

1 All of us have had something happen—little or big—one day on the way to school. Think back and recall something. It does not have to be anything dramatic. Any little thing would do. It would be interesting if you give the details, not if you try to exaggerate things like those third class shows on television. So try to remember all the details of the place, the persons involved, the conversation, and so on. What you cannot actually remember you must make up in your imagination.

Then write the story of the scene, putting in those details of what happened that will make a reader of your story live through the experience as you felt it. Write like Michael Anthony.

Give your story a title that you think is interesting and suitable.

2 Think of a market—the vendors, the stalls, the sounds, the crowd, the movement, the things on sale, the smells, and so on.

Imagine a little boy or girl wandering around in it, seeing things as a little boy or girl would, listening, looking, thinking, feeling. He or she sees some mangoes or bananas or some other fruit and would like very much to get some. But he (she) finds out that he (she) does not have enough money.

Make up an ending for the story in your mind, and then write the whole story from the beginning when he/she enters the market. If you wish you could begin with this sentence: *Les walked slowly through the wide gate of the market.* Try to write like Michael Anthony, giving lots of market details in simple sentences.

3 Try to make up a story of something that happened one day when a boy or girl like yourself went into a shopping mall or plaza or area. It might have been Christmas time and there were pick-pockets around, or it might have been a time when only a few people were shopping and the pavement vendors were trying to get the few passers-by to buy things.

Imagine the boy or girl having a happy experience with some person or persons there and write the story narrating the scene of what you imagine happened.

3 THE INTERLUDE
Michael Anthony

Tuning in

Sometimes a person cannot get away from what he or she did in the past because other persons remember and behave as if the past must not ever die. In this story, *The Interlude*, Michael Anthony of Trinidad tells of some events he imagined could have taken place in a few minutes when someone's past deeds caused something to happen.

The train raced in at sundown. It hustled forward maddeningly along the rails, and when it came to the North Bend it seemed to scream as it hugged the curving yard lines. And after the North Bend there was the town a little way in the distance. The train seemed to run
5 on the very edge of the seawall and on the other side, the rows of railway buildings and repair yards and old locomotives whizzed by.

Then the train gave a loud whistle as it passed the signalbox and after that there were a few jerks and the carriages began slowing down.
10 Passengers put their heads out of the windows to look at the town. Some of them had left San Fernando only that morning. Some had been away for weeks. Willis held the brown paper parcel under his arm and stared at the railway station and at the red houses that stretched away to the hills. Then he walked stiffly to the other side of
15 the train and he looked at the jetty and at the motor-launches out in the gulf. He had not seen San Fernando for two years.

The carriages made bigger jerks now and the rows of railway buildings and old locomotives passed by more slowly. And presently they entered the great arch of the railway station and they came to the
20 platforms with the train crawling to a stop. Willis watched the crowds on the platform and shrank back a little. It seemed almost the same crowd that had lined the platform when he was taken away. Then he was hustled between two policemen and put quickly into the small cross-barred compartment. But the crowd had still seen him and had
25 raised their voices and has used insulting words. And he was even as hostile as they and wanted to shout back. But the policemen had pushed him forward and there was a truncheon against the small of his back.

He pulled his hat right down over his eyes. He was not hostile now
30 but ashamed and a little afraid. Two years was a long time. He didn't think of the soreness of his body. Because whether you were meek or you were difficult it made no difference to the warders. One just had

no right to be behind bars. That was the warders' reasoning. Maybe they were right. He was a little afraid because he didn't want to be
35 behind bars any more. He hoped they would leave him alone now. In a town, once you lived meekly no one troubled you. But once the gang knew you they did not leave you alone. It did not matter whether you had changed or not. They did not realise two years was a long time to think. Then, too, though the other people never troubled you, once
40 they heard you made two years for wounding they kept away from you and walked on the other side of the road. It didn't matter to them whether you were a new man or not. The carriages clanged against each other and jerked to a stop. The crowd was thick on the platform. Willis pulled his hat deeper over his eyes and his mind was really
45 troubled. He wasn't sure that he should have come back to this town.

Two years made a strange difference to the appearance of San Fernando. The town seemed more open, more spread out. Everything, in fact, looked more spread out. Maybe it was because the world had suddenly broken loose from the limits of a six by six cell.
50 The fear in Willis' heart had died down. He had walked through the crowd on the platform and onto the wharf and no one had taken notice of him. No one whispered to the other and said, Look . . . He had watched their mouths and their eyes but none took notice of him. They had forgotten about him. Perhaps some knew. And perhaps
55 they pretended to forget because they had forgiven. Maybe he will be able to settle down and live in peace. Maybe . . . And then he thought of the gang. They were desperadoes. There was nothing on the face of the earth they would leave alone. He knew, because he had been a desperado too. They knew him as 'The Tiger'. But now the tiger in
60 him was tamed. It was two years he had been up for. It seemed an eternity. He wondered if they were tamed too.

He remembered what Little John had shouted to him after the sentence. They were leading him away then. Little John had shouted 'We'll get you—if we have to wait ten years we'll get you!'
65 And he had swung round in anger and had shaken his handcuffs and had said 'Watch yourself, Little John. Watch yourself!' And the people had laughed because he had shaken his handcuffs and the police had pushed him forward savagely, then looked round to see who was trifling with the law. Then he was driven away to the train station.
70 That was two years ago but it seemed like twenty. It seemed long because in jail it took so much to see a day out. It took hunger and the shouts of the warders and it took brutality and a lot of pain.

He wondered if Little John had any ideas about that. Little John liked to talk loudly from the corners of his mouth, and he liked to
75 know he was bad, but he had never been to jail. But two years was enough time to cool any man down. He hoped Little John had forgotten things by now. For after a man had been through two years

of what he, Willis, had been through, he only wanted to come back to his own little town and live in peace.

80   Willis walked slowly, his parcel under his arm, looking at the openness and the wideness of the town. He looked too at the many people whom he knew and who just passed him by. He was glad they passed him by like that and yet he wondered if they really forgot. He hoped they did and yet he didn't know that he should. They looked so

85 warm and friendly. He was glad he came back. He walked up St Vincent Street and he stopped at an orange-vendor's stall to refresh himself.

    In the town the gang had talked among themselves. For the past few days they had been talking. They knew that the Tiger was going to be

90 uncaged and they were afraid. All except Little John. When he had said he would get the Tiger he was not only playing brave. He had meant it. For Little John was a real desperado and bravado and not like the rest. Many of the gang carried knives and ice-picks and talked from the sides of their mouths but they'd run if a leaf trembled in the dark.

95 Little John feared nothing. Not even the Tiger. There were times when the Tiger had run wild, and had sliced up many of the gang and had got away with it. Some of them carried his trade mark on their bellies and on their cheeks and behind their ears. But not Little John. He and the Tiger had never clashed but he knew who would carry the

100 mark if they did. He knew one of them was going to carry some mark soon. He had waited two years for that. The Tiger must not hold the town at bay any more. He had ambushed Cyril and had used his knife in such a manner that now Cyril was crippled for good. And he had made only two years for that. If the Tiger was allowed back in the

105 town it would be another reign of terror. The rest of the gang would be finished up too. Because they were already afraid. But he, Little John, was not afraid. He had stayed there and fumed and boiled up for two years, waiting for the Tiger to be let loose.

    And now the train had come in he had felt all his strength, and the

110 lion was awake in him. He had stood in the crowd and had seen the man with the brown paper parcel under his arm step down onto the platform. His heart had pounded. And impatiently he had followed him along the wharf. There was a certain arrogance in the way the Tiger had ambled on. As if the town was his and he had come back to

115 rule it again. Little John had walked behind him impatiently knowing that sooner or later he must accost him. He mustn't give him a chance to get his balance. He mustn't let him settle down.

    And now up St Vincent Street the Tiger had stood up at an orange-stall, peeling and sucking oranges. This riled Little John even

120 more. Prison had seemed to give this man the easy cool confidence of hardened criminals. He was standing casually to suck oranges in the town where many carried the marks of his knife and where he had

butchered one so mercilessly that he was now crippled for good. Bitterness swelled in Little John. Now was the time to act. He put his hand into his pocket. The sharp point answered him. He walked out into the open. 'Tiger!' he cried 'Tiger!' And the way he shouted it was as if ten lions were awake in him.

Willis turned around. His heart seemed to drop down into his stomach. People passing in the street stopped to look. They looked at Willis and whispered to each other that this was the man. Little John stood there defiant, raging. No, they didn't forget in this town. No one did. There were more people in the street now. The orange-vendor stared at the man at his stall. The word 'Tiger' had put a fearful doubt in him. Little John advanced a step or two. The orange-vendor grew nervous. There seemed to be trouble brewing. Willis looked at the crowd and looked at Little John advancing. The crowd glared hostilely at him and he knew he couldn't run. There was no avoiding the trouble. And he remembered the two years he had just had and for once he was really afraid.

'Alright, Little John,' he said. 'What wrong boy, what wrong wid you?'

'What wrong wid me?' Little John screamed back. 'You think I is Cyril? You think you could do me what you do Cyril? You can't threaten me, Tiger. You can't threaten me and get away. Is either I mince you up or you mince me up!'

'Call the Police,' the orange-vendor cried, 'Somebody go and call the Police!'

Little John was already across the road. There was no way out for Willis. The Tiger, who had so long kept the town at bay was now at bay. He saw the flash of an ice-pick and Little John lunged towards him. Swiftly Willis ducked away, shielding his face. And as his face turned he saw the long sharp blade of the orange-vendor among the oranges. And in that moment of desperation he whipped it from the tray. He was ferocious. He was the terrible Tiger again. He caught hold of Little John's arm on the swing and brought him crashing to the pavement. Then he drove the orange-knife in the soft place between the ribs. Blood spouted out. The crowd was haywire now. The policemen pushed their way through the crowd throwing people aside. Two or three of them held the Tiger, locking his arms behind his back. And they chucked him along to the Black Maria and drove off.

Talking about it

A   The events of the story

1   *Two years was a long time.* (l.30). Where had Willis been for two years?
2   By what other name was Willis called? Why?
3   What things did Willis notice after leaving the train?
4   Who was Little John?
5   Why did Little John wait at the railway station to see Willis?
6   What change did Willis want to make in his life?
7   What happened to Little John?
8   What do you think the Black Maria is?
9   What do you suppose happened to Willis afterwards?
10 What is the interlude that the title refers to?

B   The writing skills

1   Do you think the author wants you to be sorry for Willis, or to be against him?
2   Which one of these do you think best describes the theme of the story, and why?

   a) ambition   b) loneliness   c) revenge   d) carelessness

3   Would you say the story is quite believable, or is it unlikely to happen and hard to believe?
4   How does the author seem to regard warders in a prison?
5   What is there about the style or way the writer uses language to remind you of detective stories or crime stories on television?
6   Characters in stories are described as *flat* characters or *round* characters. A *flat character* is one that you only know one side of. A *round character* is one that you know more than one side of. Would you say the characters in *The Interlude* are *flat*, or *round*?
7   Things that happen in a gripping way are said to be dramatic, but if they are much too dramatic we describe them as *melodramatic*. How would you describe *The Interlude, dramatic* or *melodramatic*?
8   What Willis did in the past causes his downfall just as he had made up his mind to become a changed and better person. It was too late. That is an example of what is called *irony*. Some people would say Willis was the victim of an irony of fate. Would you agree that it is also *ironic* that this time he was only defending himself?
9   Where does the writer give details of the scene to help readers to imagine it fully?

10 Certain parts of stories are written like this:

In the town the gang had talked among themselves. For the past few days they had been talking. They knew that the Tiger was going to be uncaged and they were afraid.

In fiction, that way of telling or narrating what happened is called *summary*.

Other parts of stories are written like this:

Willis walked slowly, his parcel under his arm, looking at the openness and wideness of the town. He looked too at the many people whom he knew and who just passed him by.

In fiction, that way of telling or narrating what happened is called *scene*.

Try really to understand the difference between *scene* and *summary* writing, and point out two places in *The Interlude* where a *scene*, is presented, and two places where *summary* is given.

C *The use of words*

1 The words in italics are used in the story. Look back at how each one is used, make a thoughtful guess about its meaning, and then discuss which one of the other words in the same row is nearest in meaning to it.

interlude   attack   promise   interval   arrival
hustled (l.23)   covered   hurried   sewn   tied
crippled (l.123)   maimed   roasted   angry   alone
ambled (l.114)   ran   talked   sang   walked
trifling (l.69)   eating   shooting   joking   carving
brutality (l.72)   silence   cruelty   ignorance   clumsiness
arrogance (l.113)   conceit   beauty   weakness   fear

2 Here are some other words used in the story. Look back at how each one is used and make a thoughtful guess about its meaning.

hostile (l.26)   *meek* (l.31)   *bravado* (l.92)   *fumed* (l.107)
accost (l.116)   *riled* (l.119)   *casually* (l.121)   *defiant* (l.131)
glared (l.136)   *desperation* (l.153)   *ferocious* (l.154)

Now discuss which one of them best fits into each blank space in this paragraph.

The leader of the gang was _____ by the girl's _____ behaviour. He expected her to be _____ and humble, but she just _____ at him and _____ turned her back, as he became more _____ , threatening her with punishment. As he _____ in his rage and nothing happened he seemed to reach a point of _____ and attempted to _____ her. But she let loose a _____ barrage of blows upon him like a karate expert and all of his _____ turned to cowering.

Beaming out

In your spare time this week try to do one of these and keep it in your folder to show whoever you wish.

1 Think of a time in your life when you felt very hurt by someone and felt like doing something to get revenge. Write the story of what happened to make you feel that way.

2 Describe a dramatic scene (remember how to write *scene*) between two people who have been friends for a long time, but now one accuses the other of something that might make them enemies.

3 Make up a round character who is very sorry about some things he or she did in the past and wants to do something now to make up for those wrongdoings.

    Write the story of an incident when he or she tried to show the change of heart but was ironically accused of a wrongdoing.

4 Imagine or recall an occasion when you went to a district or town or village that you hadn't known before or hardly knew.

    Narrate your thoughts as you walked or drove through the place looking at people and things.

4 ALLELUIA MORNING
John Wickham

Tuning in

Sometimes a story is made up about a very strange person or a very strange idea. And sometimes that makes it hard to believe. See whether you find it easy or difficult to believe in the mother and daughter in this story.

(*Skyscrapers* are very tall buildings hundreds of metres high. An *accompanist* is a person who plays a piano or other musical instrument to accompany a singer. A *recital* is a concert put on by a singer, choir, dancers or musicians. *Sophistication* is knowledge and experience of the world. *Subtle* means not easy to see or separate).

———

'Good morning, Miss Morning.'
The voices, the village voices echo through the open window, through the early morning mist, past the tops of the skyscrapers and enter the room.

'Good morning, Miss Morning, Miss Morning, Miss Morning.'

The voices sing diminuendo, sing in the morning as their owners, so many mornings ago, pass outside my mother's window and find the song in her name impossible to resist.

'Good morning, Miss Morning,' sang the men and women, the boys and the girls, big and small, in my village, in greeting and now, hundreds of mornings after, high in a room in a great city where no one sings in greeting in the morning, I hear the singing voices again. They are always singing and I have only to pause and be still to hear them like rain hushing the trees far away or the sea sobbing against the shoulder of the shore.

I know no one with a name like mine. I have never heard of anyone called Morning, only my mother and me. I did not know my father and when I used to ask my mother about him, all she would say was, 'My dear, he died one morning.' A conundrum, that reply, whose meaning is not yet clear.

'Your name,' my mother told me, 'is your name. It is Alleluia Morning.'

'What is your name?' my mother asked me, over and over, again and again. And again and again I would have to say my name like a lesson learnt by heart, like the answer to two and two.

'Alleluia Morning,' I would say, 'Alleluia Morning is my name.'

'Sing it, child, sing it,' my mother commanded me.

And I sang my name 'Alleluia Morning' every morning, noon and

night. I sang my name as I used to hear everyone in the village singing
it.

'Sing your name at the top of your voice,' my mother said to me. 'It
is yours and no one can take it from you unless you want them to. It
may be all you have, but it is yours.'

And I sang my name, Alleluia Morning, at the top of my voice.
'Why did you give me that name?' I asked my mother.

'Because I was glad when you were born,' she said. 'Because you
were as welcome as a blessing I cried 'Alleluia' when you were born.'

I loved my name and used to sing it and hear it singing in my ears
and the sound of it made me glad because I was a blessing to my
mother. And, in truth, there was never another name as beautiful as
my name and there was a time when I would feel sorry for the Glorias
and the Dorothys and Helens and Joans and Josephines and Marys
because their names were not as sweet as mine, Alleluia Morning.

When I was going off to school, my mother spoke to me again. She
charged me not to lose my name.

'Your books, your slate, your pencil, the ribbons in your hair, lose
them, throw them away if you like but never play careless with
Alleluia Morning. It is all that you have. Don't put it down carelessly
and forget it and don't let anyone steal it from you.'

'And why,' I asked my mother, 'should anyone steal my name from
me?' I laughed. I could not think what a person could do with a stolen
name. But my mother was cross with me. She felt I was making fun of
her.

'Because,' she said when I had stopped laughing, 'because people
are like that. They will steal it because they think it is too good for you
and after they have stolen it they will throw it away, on the stuff heap,
because they will not know what to do with it. And it will rust and rot
so that in the end it will be of no use to you or to them.'

And I went off to school with my mother's warning ringing and my
name singing in my ears, Alleluia Morning.

'Good morning, children,' my teacher said.

'Good morning, teacher,' the children sang.

'Names, please,' the teacher said.

And one by one, we sang our names to the teacher. Alice and Mary
and Belle and Grace, Judy, Jenny, Germaine, Violet, Frances, Flavia,
Doreen and Delcina and Flora and Eileen and Joyce and Maria. And
then, 'Alleluia, teacher, Alleluia Morning.'

'What?' asked the teacher. She could not believe what she had heard.
And so, remembering what my mother had told me, I sang my name,
I sang it at the top of my voice.

'Alleluia Morning,' I sang.

'What a strange name,' the teacher said and the girls giggled.

'I have never heard a name like that before,' the teacher said and the girls giggled even more.

'Are you sure that's your name?' the teacher asked and the girls burst out in giggles so loud that she could not hear me when I said that I was sure that it was my name, because my mother had given it to me.

'That's enough, girls,' the teacher said.

'Is that your real name?' she asked quietly and in a very kind voice.

The girls were all quiet and listening when I told the teacher again and I was sure that my real name was Alleluia Morning because my mother gave it to me when I was born.

'It is a very pretty name,' the teacher said. And I told her that I knew that it was pretty because my mother had warned me to be very careful with it and not to lose it as it was all I had.

That day the girls gathered around me in the playground.

'What is your name?' they asked.

'Alleluia Morning,' I said.

'Your real name?' They did not believe.

'Yes,' I crossed my heart and hoped to die, 'my real name.'

'Say it again,' they begged, 'we have never heard such a name before.'

And I sang my name as my mother had taught me. Over and over again I sang my name.

'Alleluia Morning, Alleluia Morning.'

One girl said, 'Let us call her Allie. That's shorter and nicer.' And they all said together, 'Yes, let's call her Allie, that's shorter and nicer.'

I understood that they wanted to be friends, that they meant kindness and I nearly said, I was on the edge of saying, 'All right, I don't mind, you can call me Allie if you wish. That's shorter.' But then I remembered what my mother had told me, how she had warned me not to let anyone play games with my name, nor take it from me, nor rob me of any part of it. And so, although I knew that my new friends meant kindness by calling me 'Allie', I said that my name was 'Alleluia' and I would prefer it if they called me by my right name. And I told them what my mother had said, that when I was born, she was glad and said, 'Alleluia' and that I was to take care of my name as long as I lived. And the girls laughed and one or two of them began to tease me by singing 'Allie, Allie, Alleluia, Allie, Allie, Alleluia,' but although I knew that they were not going to steal my name, I knew too that I had to be careful, for without meaning to, they might break my name, as sometimes I had broken a glass or saucer just through carelessness, and all I cried afterwards was never enough to mend the broken thing again. So, although I knew they meant no harm by their 'Allie, Allie, Alleluia,' I cried out to them.

'No, no,' I cried, 'my name is Alleluia, my name is Alleluia.'

'But we are only making fun,' the girls said, 'We know your name is Alleluia. It is a very pretty name.'

31

'Then call me by my very pretty name,' I said.

And the girls said, 'All right, all right then, we'll call you by your name but we were only making fun.'

'But you said,' I reminded them, 'that Alleluia is a very pretty name.'

'All right,' they said, 'Alleluia.'

My mother was right. I had to be on guard always. Oh, the tricks they used to try to rob me of my name.

The tricks of the devil, as my mother had told me. The girls meant no harm but the result would have been malicious. I grew bigger and went to another school and there, at first, they tried to make me ashamed of my name so that I would put it away for myself. They called me 'Morning,' 'Afternoon,' 'A.M.,' 'Forenoon,' 'Fore-day Morning,' everything but my real name, 'Alleluia Morning.' It was not easy. Many times I was tempted to forget my mother's charge and say, 'Let them call me whatever they like. They can't change the real me. I am what I am. After all, what's in a name?' But I always heard my mother's voice singing 'Alleluia' in my ears.

'Sing your name, sing it out at the top of your voice.' My mother's voice rang out. 'You are a blessing and I called you 'Alleluia'.' And, hearing my mother's voice, I would be strong enough to turn on the temptation and say 'My name is Alleluia Morning.'

And gradually, always after I had shown how stubborn I was over my name, stubborn and over-sensitive and wearing a chip on my shoulder and all the other fancy words they gave to my simple wish to be called by no other name than the name my mother gave me, reluctantly they would give in and say, 'All right then, your name is Alleluia Morning.'

The tricks were legion. What kind of a name is that? A peasant name, a name from the backwoods, a slave's name, a name without sophistication, a made-up name, a false name, no name at all. But the subtlest, the cleverest trick of all was played when I came to this great city to study and to sing.

'Oh!' they cried, 'Alleluia Morning, what a beautiful name!' Tutor, music-master, professor, accompanist, all of them, with one voice, cried 'What a beautiful name!' they clapped their hands, delighted, and said, 'A beautiful name to match a beautiful voice.'

And I was glad that at last, far from home, strangers recognised how beautiful my name was. I was happy and said to myself, 'I could live here contented forever among these kind people who are so quick to see and acknowledge how beautiful my name is. They are truly what they say they are, civilised and cultivated and humanist and without prejudice and may indeed be the chosen people of heaven.' I was so happy that I sang like a bird, from recital to recital and from concert to concert. From town to town, all over the country, from shore to shore, my name sang 'Alleluia Morning'. The headlines of newspapers carried my name, the radio sang it, the records multiplied and everywhere I went I heard myself singing. I sang like a blessing, like a bird, they said, and I was happier than I had ever thought I should be.

Moreover, my mother, far away, was happy too. She wrote each week to tell me what a gladness it gave her that I was singing in the big country and that I was truly a blessing. She heard my voice sometimes and she was so happy when she did that she could not help crying. But, she warned me, she would never grow tired of warning me, I was never to forget to guard my name: I was not to be careless with it. Remember, she wrote, remember and have a care.

Last night I sang before the greatest crowd of all, in the greatest hall in this great city. Rows and rows of people sat before me and when I sang for them they shouted, they clapped their hands and cried 'Bravo, bravo!' at the tops of their voices. And I sang again and again and yet again and the more I sang the more they wanted me to sing. In the end, when, unwillingly, they stopped clapping and went away, I sat in the dressing-room before the mirror, among the red roses and the yellow roses and the gladioli and all the many-coloured flowers of tribute and triumph. Admiration was all around me. I felt myself floating on the voices of congratulation, high above the hands outstretched to touch, the programmes offered for autographs, the adoration, the sweet adoration. And the newspaper critics, the music men, all flattering and courteous. I knew them all. They had all been kind to me for many years and many concerts and some of them had predicted that one day I should have such a success as this. I knew them all except one. There was a young, fresh-faced handsome one, with the whiskers of the moment's fashion and a furtive smile curving around the corners of his mouth. I had never seen him before.

He caught me looking at him. 'Miss Morning,' he said, offering his hand in greeting, his eyes also offering his tribute of praise and congratulation, 'that was the finest singing I have ever heard.'

I thanked him. 'I have to write it up,' he said, 'and I don't know what to say.'

I was touched. I had never, I thought, been paid such a compliment.

'But, tell me, Miss Morning,' the young man was saying, 'I hope I don't seem rude, but is your name really Alleluia Morning?'

'Yes,' I said, after a while, a long while, 'it really is.'

'Thank you, Miss Morning,' The young man bowed politely and turned on his heels and shoved his way through the throng to the door.

The newspapers carry my picture this morning and my name is in headlines. Alleluia Morning, the newspapers shout, a triumph! A voice like a blessing! A glad voice! The banners scream.

Below one headline my eyes catch the words '. . . continues to
210 insist that her real name is Alleluia Morning. If it is, then never was a
name more proper.'

My mother was right, is right. You cannot be careless, there are all
sorts of tricks to rob you of your name.

Talking about it

A *The events of the story*

1   *The village voices echo through the open window* (1.2). Where is
    Alleluia at the time?

    a) *at school*   b) *in her village*   c) *in a big city*

2   What did Alleluia's mother tell her about her name?
3   How seriously did Alleluia take her mother's words about her
    name?
4   In what way did the girls at her first school behave towards
    Alleluia?
5   What happened with the children at her second school?
6   What did Alleluia do for a living when she grew up?
7   Why was Alleluia *far from home* (1.156)?
8   Who was the *young, fresh-faced handsome one* (1.191), and why did he
    go to Alleluia?
9   To be *civilised* (1.160) means a lot more than not being a savage and
    eating one another. Who are the people described as *civilised and
    cultivated and humanist* (1.160), and why are they so described?

B *The writing skills*

1   What do you enjoy most or least about the story?
2   Suppose Alleluia was not given that name would the rest of the
    story have had to be different?
3   Do you think the story is convincingly told, in a way that makes it
    easy for you to believe it?
4   Can you find a part of the story that may be described as *scene*, and
    part that may be described as *summary*?
5   A *flashback* is a part of a story or film where it goes back to
    something that happened earlier. Does *Alleluia Morning* have a
    flashback?
6   Which character is the rounder character in the story, Alleluia or
    her mother?

7   Which one of these phrases do you think best describes the *style* (the way the writer used language) in the story?

   a)   dull and heavy
   b)   fast and exciting
   c)   simple and childlike
   d)   difficult and pompous

C   *The use of words*

1   Here are some words used in the story. Look back at how each one is used, make a thoughtful guess about its meaning, and discuss which of the sentences below it best fits into.

   mist (1.3)   *resist* (1.8)   *malicious* (1.128)   *sensitive* (1.142)
   stubborn (1.141)   *reluctantly* (1.145)   *triumph* (1.184)   *outstretched*
   (1.185)   *furtive* (1.192)   *throng* (1.204)

   a)   With arms _____ he embraced his two children.
   b)   Kate's refusal to agree showed us how _____ she was.
   c)   In the early morning a thin _____ covers the hills.
   d)   A restless _____ of people was waiting to get into the store.
   e)   She was very _____ about how she was spoken to.
   f)   I felt like laughing but was able to _____ the urge.
   g)   When Bunty saw that Fay was serious he _____ went and picked up the 'phone.
   h)   On hearing that he had won Michael danced around the room in _____ .
   i)   Floria had a _____ look on her face and I knew she was going to do something wicked.
   j)   The two men crept around the building in such a _____ way that I knew they were up to no good.

2   Make your own oral sentences using these words, after thinking about how they are used in the story.

   echo (1.2)   *conundrum* (1.19)   *giggled* (1.72)   *prefer* (1.105)
   gradually (1.141)   *recognised* (1.156)   *acknowledge* (1.159)
   prejudice (1.161)   *adoration* (1.187)   *tribute* (1.195)   *predicted* (1.190)
   compliment (1.199)

Beaming out

Do one of these or anything else in your spare time this week and keep it in your folder for showing to others:

1   Children sometimes tease one another by using hurtful
    nicknames. Can you remember anyone who was teased in that
    way? If you can, try to make up a story in very simple language
    about an occasion when he or she was teased by a group of
    children.
2   Imagine that you were an internationally known singer or dancer
    or musician, and you were in a big city to give a concert or recital.
    Make up an incident that took place after the concert or recital and
    write a clear account of it, as *scene*, not as *summary*.
3   Make up a character who has a very strange view of things.
    Suppose that one day that person gets into a situation where he or
    she has to choose between keeping friends and sticking to his or
    her opinion.

    Try to imagine the scene as clearly as you can and then write it
    with all the details that would make it seem real.

5 WHAT'S UP, PARDNER?
Cecil Gray

Tuning in

Did you ever meet a person who did not want to get close to or take anyone into his or her heart? Did you ever wonder why a person might get like that? Do you think such a person can change? In this story, Darma has to make a choice.

(A *routine* is a set of actions done over and over again in the same order.)

———

There are shouts of children playing the street but Darma does not hear. She never hears the sound of children's voices any more. The shrieks hardly reach her in her closed-up world and she is satisfied. She does not want to be Darma to anyone else but her daughter and
5　son-in-law now. To let herself hear the voices would be to become a grandmother again, to be called Darma again by some two year-old who could not say Grandma. She doesn't want that. She tries to shut out the voices from outside as she walks very slowly from the sink to the window drying her teacup. There is no need for hurry. She pulls
10　the pale blue curtain a little, telling herself how irritating it is to have these children around. She peeks through the curtain at them.

The neighbours' two boys and the other two from across the road are screaming at one another in cowboy language, shooting bang! bang! and dropping suddenly dead for a moment or two. She remem-
15　bers a little how she too squealed and shouted and banged and raced, such a long, long time ago it seems now. So much has happened since. The mother of the boys across the road comes up and calls out something to her boys. They rush to her and hug her and pull her and jump around her. Darma recalls how her own three boys and two girls
20　gambolled around her when they were that age. The boys were all sturdy and she had to warn them to be more gentle with her. The girls had beautiful eyes and teeth, and dimples like her own mother used to have. Those were the days of living, the days of happiness. Now her comfort is in the unbroken routine she follows, living with her
25　daughter and son-in-law.

She had always said how lucky she was to be able to live with them. They had no children although they had been married for nearly ten years and the house was never racked by a child's laughter nor disturbed in its pattern by a child's frisky games. Darma filled each day
30　with the same tasks and on most evenings looked at television even though the programmes were all trash. It helped to pass the time. Sometimes she wondered if living meant just passing the time, but she

always reminded herself that she did not need to enjoy life anymore, or to let new things into her life, but just to keep on in her set ways
35 until the end.

She turned away from the window and put down the cup on the dresser and she suddenly remembered the present. The clock struck four. Soon Carol and David would be walking into the house with a stranger. Soon all that she had grown accustomed to would have to
40 change. And there was nothing she could do about it. After all, if they wanted to adopt a child they were entitled to do so. They must have longed for one for years. She was not going to stand in their way. But she was not going to take any strange little boy as her own either. They knew very well that when Bruce, her only grandson, died
45 something inside her died with him, that she couldn't find it in her heart to laugh and play with children any more. But this strange boy would be their son. She didn't have to do more than be polite to him. She definitely did not want him to call her Darma as Bruce did. Bruce had named her Darma as soon as he began to talk. No one else must
50 use Bruce's name for her.

'Here we are!' Darma was startled at the sound of Carol's happy voice. She hadn't heard them open the gate. Now there they stood: Carol, David and a little sturdy boy of eight with bright eyes and a round, happy face. 'Here he is, mother.' Carol was beaming. David
55 had an anxious smile sculpted on his face. The strange boy stared at her with his bright eyes.

'I can see,' Darma said.

'Isn't he adorable?' Carol said.

Darma didn't answer.

60 Carol turned to the boy. 'Go and wash your face, darling. Daddy will show you where.' Father and son bounded down the passage, the boy splitting the air with his laughter.

'Mother, you promised not to behave badly about this.'

'Now, what did I do?'

65 'It's what you didn't do. You've got to get to know him and he has to get to know you and the quicker the better. Tell you what, why don't you go for the milk today and take him along with you?'

Darma did not want to be troublesome; far from it. It was only that she felt they were not fair in expecting her to show love to some
70 strange little boy from a Home just because they had decided to adopt him. But she wanted to be as co-operative as she could manage to be.

'All right, all right,' she said. 'But don't expect me to giggle with him.' She sat and waited for David and the boy to come back. She knew it would happen that way, that new and upsetting things would
75 spoil everything for her. She had never gone to fetch the milk from the grocery shop. Now she was as much as ordered to do it—and with a noisy little brat from a Home where children had no parents and no

discipline. She wondered what would happen next.

Not once during that errand did Darma utter a word. Not once did
anything like a smile cross her rigid features. The boy trotted alongside. At first he seemed afraid. Then he gradually seemed to grow less
distant, less shy as they walked briskly along. He said things more to
himself than to the old lady—things about the cars, the buildings, the
people. Darma scarcely heard him.

They got back to the house and time passed heavily until they all sat
down for supper. All through the meal Darma could hear, though she
tried not to, David and Carol telling their new-found intruder about
themselves and about the neighbourhood and what things they were
going to do for him. He smiled and chuckled and shouted with
delight—at the pleasures they promised. Darma felt it was not right.
After all, he was not a real member of the family. He couldn't take
Bruce's place. Carol and David were being very stupid.

After supper Darma did not stay to watch television. 'I have some
knitting to do,' she told Carol and went into her room. She had
scarcely begun to knit when she heard the restless ball of mischief
exploring the house and yelling with joy at things he saw. The lamp
behind the big green armchair was declared a 'bad guy' with a striped
hat. And under the old round table in the corner the 'bad guy' had his
hide-out for rounding up his gang of teddy bears. Darma was
suddenly aware that she was the spy who was signalling with Indian
smoke signs to the bad ones down in the valley. 'The spy' had to be
taken by surprise. He approached her stealthily.

'What's up, pardner?' he demanded.

'I beg your pardon. Did you say "pardner"? Don't you know the
word is partner?' Darma spoke sternly, pointing her knitting needle at
the would-be cowboy. Suddenly the gunman swung round and shot
twice at the lamp with his fat little fingers. Then he screamed and
crumpled up on the floor like one dying in pain. Darma gasped in
astonishment. Then a frightening alarm seized her. She rushed over to
the child. Was something the matter? Should she call for the others?

Slowly the boy's face broke into the widest, sweetest grin one could
imagine and the space where his front teeth were missing gaped
comically at her. Gradually but surely Darma's face lit up into a
beaming smile of relief and understanding. She couldn't help it. She
smiled and smiled. Then she became serious again and took up her
knitting. It was very strange, she thought. For years she had given
only a nod and a false smile to everyone. Now she had really smiled.

The little boy kept on looking at her knitting. Then he spoke.

'They went away,' he said. 'The creases in your face all went away
when you smiled. You looked like the teddy bear they gave me at the
Home one Christmas. It was the best teddy bear in the world. I used to
love it because it loved me. I could tell because its eyes were always

smiling. One day somebody stole it away. I wish I had another teddy
bear like him. His name was Dunks.'

125 'Oh?' Darma said. 'And what is your name?'

'My name at the Home was Bobby but my new Mummy and
Daddy think they want to change it. That would be good if it changed
every thing as your face changed when you smiled.'

'Yes, son. Sometimes change is necessary. What about if we call
130 you Bruce Richard Gordon? Would you like to be called Bruce? I had a
grandson who was named Bruce, but one day he was stolen away like
your teddy bear.'

'That's a nice name. Yes, I would like to be Bruce if you want me to.
And what would I call you, grandma or grannie or grandmother or
135 what?'

'Just call me Darma, Bruce. Just call me Darma.'

'Tell me about the real Bruce, Darma.'

'The real Bruce? You are the real Bruce now. But one day when you
are grown up I'll tell you about the other things.'

140 'Are you going to be with me until I grow up, Darma?'

'Well, I certainly intend to be, Bruce, and I can tell you I am a
determined woman. Come, let us go and tell Mummy and Daddy that
Bruce has come home.'

Talking about it

A *The events of the story*

1 How did Darma feel about what her daughter and son-in-law had
decided? Why?
2 Why do you suppose Darma found the shouts of the children
irritating (l.10)?
3 Who was Bruce and what had happened to him?
4 What game was Bobby playing when he said '*What's up, pardner?*'?
5 What fooled Darma and got her alarmed?
6 Why did Darma smile at Bobby as she used to smile before?
7 What tells you that Darma had really changed in her feelings about
Bobby?
8 What sort of things do you think Darma and Bobby did together
after that day?

B *The writing skills*

1 Do you find the way the writer uses language in the story (the *style*)
simple and clear or complicated and difficult? Why?
2 Read the parts where there is conversation or dialogue in the story

and discuss whether those parts are written as *scene* or as *summary*.

3 Is the third paragraph of the story written as *scene* or as *summary*?
4 Do you know enough of Darma to say that she is a *round character*?
5 Do you think the little boy, Bobby, is speaking in the story as a little boy would speak, or is that a fault in the story?
6 Do you find the story convincing or believable? Do you believe Darma would change so easily? Why or why not?
7 We say someone is *sentimental* when he or she shows more feeling for something than it should get. Do you think Darma is sentimental?
8 Do you think the story itself is a sentimental one, and that the writer wants you to feel more than you should about the situation?

C *The use of words*

1 Here are some descriptive words that were used in the story. Use each one in an oral sentence of your own.

   shriek peek squeal gambolled frisky trotted briskly chuckled yelling gasped gaped comically

2 In each row below there is a word that is out of place. Discuss why it is out of place.

   a) errand task chore underground
   b) strong bright sturdy durable
   c) deserved entitled bounded worth
   d) alarm bring get fetch
   e) rigid stiff inflexible pattern
   f) surprise astonishment amazement relief
   g) joy pleasure discipline delight
   h) intruder stranger outsider ogre

3 The word *disturb* is related in meaning to the word *disturbance*, and the word *routine* is related in meaning to the word *route*.

   Suggest at least one other word related in meaning to each of these:

   sculpted (l.55) *adopt* (l.41) *exploring* (l.96) *stealthily* (l.102)
   relief (l.114) *determined* (l.142)

Beaming out

In your spare time this week you might want to do one of these and put it into your folder to share with others, if you wish.

1   Think of an old person that you know—someone of about seventy years of age—and try to imagine what problem or problems he or she might have. Then use your imagination to make up an occasion in your mind when something happened to make a change in that person's life. Write the story of the scene in which it happened, using summary wherever you have to.
2   Try to imagine an incident one day in which a boy or girl who wanted to be taken in as a friend by a group of his or her schoolmates does something that makes them either like or dislike him or her very much.
      Write an account of the scene.

6 THE SINS OF THE FATHERS
Timothy Callender

Tuning in

Are adults always innocent of the things they forbid you to do? And would you forgive a wrong if you understood why the person did it? Perhaps you might see things as the boy in this story did, perhaps not.

Even at night, when he was lying on his bed of plaited coconut leaf, he could hear the wind, loud as in the daytime. It came wet and chilly off the sea, blew through the holes in the patched wooden walls of the tiny hut where he lived with his mother and father. When rain
5 fell he had to shift in his bed to avoid the spray which flew through the eastern wall of the hut. 'I got to fix up this house,' his father always used to say, but it never was done.

He could hear the wind in the canefields now, howling faintly, swishing along the cane-leaves and the arrows, and above it all he
10 could hear the sound of the kites. There was the loud pervading roar of the big singing-angels, the whine of the little ones swaying at the end of their thread, the flapping sound of the brownpaper bulls on the kites with single roundheads. It was like this day and night, when the kite-season came. When the Easter winds began to blow the kites
15 went up, and from then until long past Easter there would be kites in the sky, newer ones, different ones, for it was very seldom that a kite could survive the length of the Easter season. Very few flyers could preserve their kite that long. No champion could hold his title that long, though some had come fairly close. Then there were the
20 numerous mishaps that befell the kites; the electric wires, depending on where one was flying his kite, the trees, the sea, the wind itself. Kites came and went, but the kite-flying went on until, sometime around the end of April, they would all be gone.

He had never had a kite. His father had never given him one, and
25 none of the boys made kites for free. They would want six cents at least, and he never had any money. Then there was the matter of string. It was the real problem; string was expensive, his father would never give him a ball of twine. He never asked his father for a kite and twine; he had heard his mother asking in vain for too many other more
30 important things. But he had to get a kite that year, and he knew how.

He had tried chasing the kites when they broke their string, but he was no fast runner. Besides, from the time a kite broke, the alarm would be given, and so many boys would give chase that no individual could benefit from the chase; the string would have to be divided

43

35 among too many.

But he dreaded the thought of putting his idea in practice. He knew that boys had been beaten by the kiteflyers already, for trying the same thing. Not even the owner of the kite could object if his kite broke and you chased it, and claimed it as your own. It was always a matter of
40 Finders, Keepers, then. But it was something quite different to take a kite from the air. Everybody knew it was unfair simply because a flyer had no chance to save his kite; no skill in the world could stop it from coming down.

But he had long since considered the possibilities of being caught,
45 and mapped out his plan of escape. It should be fairly easy, he knew, but still he wasn't sure if he wanted to do it. And he would have to go somewhere else to fly the kite, so it wouldn't be recognised. It wouldn't be much fun flying the kite, with strange boys from another district, though. They wouldn't be friendly. They would bob your
50 cord if you went a little way away to fix your kite, you had to watch them all the time.

He lay awake thinking and listening to the kites, and around six o'clock he heard his father stir in the coconut fibre bed behind the little drape, where he slept with his mother. His father coughed and pushed
55 aside the curtain and came out. He crossed to the door and unlatched it, letting the cold light in, and he hawked and spat and held his chest for a long time, bending his head. Then he wiped his mouth and looked at his hand for a moment, stepped away from the door and moved out of the range of the boy's vision. He lay pretending to be
60 asleep and heard his father sharpening his cutlass on the hearthstone. The bed made a noise and then his mother came through the curtain and went to make the coffee for his father, and the boy continued to lie there until he smelt the coffee.

He got up and went to the hearth where the clay pot was still
65 steaming; took down a cup and dipped it full. He put in a spoonful of brown sugar and turned, sipping it, to look at his father and mother. She was standing by the door and he was sitting on the step outside, sipping from his calabash. His fishing ropes were draped around his shoulder, and his net and crocus bags were in the yard, close by his
70 feet.

'Is Good Friday,' his mother said. 'You ain't have to go out today. It ain't seem right to me.'

'What you want me to do, go to church?' his father said. He put down the calabash on the step and walked away, out of the enclosure
75 of plaited coconut leaf that formed the paling. He grew smaller as he walked down the long beach in the widening daylight, and the wind flapped the ends of his shirt.

'He is a very sick man,' his mother said, as if talking to herself. 'I don't like him alone out there in that condition. Why you don't go out

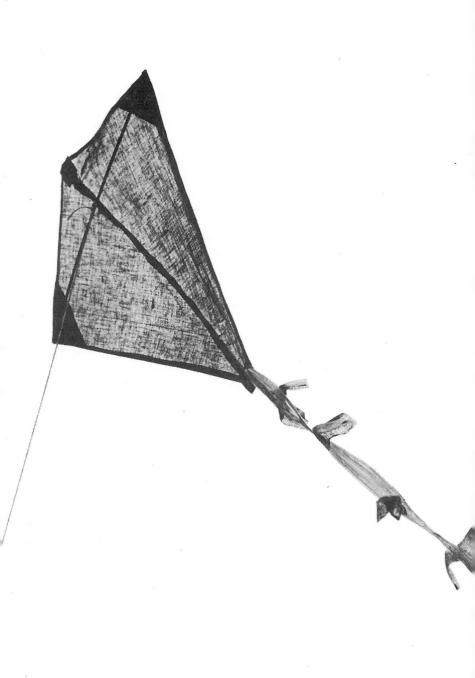

and help your father, boy? You big enough, and you know jest as much 'bout it as he. You jest good for nothing, won't hear nothin' I say at all. You want he to dead?'

He stopped drinking and stared at her.

'Good Friday,' she said. 'Easter Day two days off. And nothing at all. It going be jest like any other day.'

When she started to talk like that, he knew that he should get out of the house, else she would spend the whole day grumbling and shouting at him.

'I going get some water,' he said, and slipped outside. He took up the overturned bucket in the yard and moved away, headed for the standpipe a short distance away. As he walked, he looked up at the kites speckling the sky, hundreds and hundreds of them, he thought, and all those colours, scattered out up there, like confetti.

Later in the day, he crouched in the canefields and looked up at the kites. He had a spool of his father's fishing line, which he knew must be returned to his box before he missed it. He had tied a stone about the size of his fist to the end of the fishing line. There was a stiff piece of wire through the hole in the spool, so that it could spin freely.

Most of the kites were high, and their strings swayed, following their movements. There were no sharp tugs on their lines; they would be tied out, he knew, with nobody holding onto their string, and perhaps nobody watching the one that he was after. It was a big singing-angel with a short tail; when the wind increased it looped and swung in a wide area of sky. He could see its swizzle, two bits of glass and razor glinted on the end of its tail. As he watched, it came up roaring out of a dive, climbed high in the sky, moved sideways and hooked itself across the string of a kite even larger than itself. Its head came down and it was pulled into a dive by the pressure on its tail. The heavy cloth raked its length along the tightened string and the bigger kite snapped away, suddenly silent, and went nodding and drifting away in the distance. Already he could hear the faint shouts, 'Kite Popped!' and he saw the boys running, shouting and pointing. The wind was hard and the kite was taking long to fall and he was glad because he knew it would keep some of them occupied for a while. But he thought of all this within a second, because the swizzle-tailed kite was close to the tops of the canes, now recovering from its dive, and he jumped up and threw with all his might before it could rise. The spool jerked in his hand and the stone curved and fell, dragging the fishing line across the string. He hauled swiftly, feeling the strong pull as the kite struggled to rise, and hauled until it crashed into the canes. Then he ran forward, grabbed its string and tugged. Somewhere across the canefields, the string broke and he pulled swiftly, wrapping it around his hand as he ran stumbling through the cane clutching the kite. From afar, over the other side of the gully, boys were shouting angrily. He ran with all his might, out of the canes and over some rocks, down to the beach, to the cave he had chosen for its hiding-place.

He came home happy, sure that he had not been seen. But he had scarcely gone inside the house when he heard the voices outside, and the knock on the door.

'What wunna want?' his mother said.

'We come for we kite. Trevor have we kite. He thief it and run with it.'

'I ain't know, I ain't seen him with no kite. I ain't think he would do that. Trevor!' she called. 'These three boys out here say that you have them kite. That is true?'

Trevor looked up from where he was sitting on his bed. 'What kite? I ain't know nothing 'bout no kite.'

His mother came close and looked at him. He knew that she knew he was lying, and he looked away from her face. She stood over him, arms akimbo.

'Where the kite, Trevor? Where you put it?'

'I ain't see no kite,' he said. 'Them can't say they see me with no kite.'

'We see him,' one of the boys shouted from outside. 'We was looking at the kite through my father spying glass, and we see him close up when he was running out of the canes.'

His mother shook her head slowly, and turned to the window. 'I can't control him,' she said. 'He won't hear to me at all. You have to wait 'til his father come home this evening. Don't worry, he going have to give yuh back.'

'Huh! All right. I coming back this evening, and if I don't get it he better watch how he walking 'bout outside here. We bound to catch he sometime.' And the boys went away.

When his father came in from the sea that evening he heard the story and he didn't waste any time. 'Boy, go and get that kite from wherever you hiding it,' he said, and Trevor knew better than to argue. He went down to the cave on the beach and brought it back to the house. Then his father flogged him with his heavy canvas belt.

'I beating you because you know better than that,' he said. 'I ain't raising you up to be no thief. And you had no right telling yuh mother lies either. If you did want a kite as bad as that I woulda help get one for yuh. You didn't have to do that at all.'

And the next day his father gave him ten cents and he went at Boysie's shop and bought a beautiful round-kite. His father gave him part of an old fishnet and he unravelled it to make his twine, and he spent the whole of Easter Sunday flying his kite, except when he went home for the midday meal.

It was a special meal after all; his mother had cooked a turkey that his

170 father brought home the night before. The three of them sat in the
house and ate, enjoying it, knowing that a long time would pass
before such a treat would come their way again. His belly was full
when he returned to the gully to let out his kite again, and he flew it
there until the evening. Then, not wanting to risk leaving it out for the
175 night, he hauled it in and headed for home.

When he came into the yard he stopped in surprise. There was a
policeman standing there, and for a minute he thought that the boys
had sent him to recover their kite. But there were two other men, both
from the poultry farm a mile away—the watchman, and the man in
180 charge of the place. And then he saw his father leaning by the side of
the house and talking to them.

'It was two of wunna,' the watchman said. 'Who was the other
one?'

'You will have to find him yuhself,' his father said. 'All I can say is, I
185 really sorry and I going to pay for both of them if you want me to. I
ain't want no trouble, Mr Watson. I begging you not to take it no
further than that. Is Easter time, and everybody would want to eat at
least today.'

The boy knew at once what they were talking about, he realised
190 immediately that his father could never have bought a turkey like that.
He turned before the men saw him, came out of the yard, and walked
quickly away down the beach. He would wait until they left before he
returned. He hoped that nobody would hear about it, but he knew the
chances of secrecy were slim, the village talked too much.
195 And he was right. The other fellows knew. When he came to fly his
kite the next day, the boys were waiting to taunt him.

'Thief, thief!' they shouted. 'You and your father is the same, all o'
wunna is thieves.'

'A chip off the old block, that is what my father say. Like father, like
200 son.'

But he knew they wouldn't dare to touch him and he kept on flying
his kite. He was sure that there was a big difference between him and
his father, and he was content.

Talking about it

A *The events of the story*

1   What was the name of the person about whom the story is told?
2   What was he afraid of doing to the boys' kites!
3   The swizzle-tailed kite *hooked itself across the string of a kite even
larger than itself* (l.107). What happened to the larger kite then?

4 What did the boy do when the swizzle-tailed kite was trying to rise again from its dive?
5 What is it to stand *with arms akimbo* (1.141)?
6 What did the father do when he knew what the boy did?
7 What special meal did the father provide, and why?
8 *The boy knew at once what they were talking about* (1.189). What were they talking about?
9 *. . . the chances of secrecy were slim* (1.194). Can you say that in a different way?
10 Why did the other boys say Trevor was *a chip off the old block* (1.199)?
11 How did Trevor feel about the trouble his father was in?

B *The writing skills*

1 How does the writer get you to understand the poverty that Trevor and his parents were living in?
2 Do you think the author wants you

   a) to feel sorry for Trevor's father,
   b) to be glad that Trevor's father was arrested,
   c) to be sorry that Trevor was teased by his friends?

3 What do you think of the part Trevor's mother played in the story?
4 Is there any part of the story that you found unlikely or improbable or difficult to believe?
5 The beginning of the story is written as *summary*. Where does it change to *scene*?
6 Why do you think the title of the story is *The Sins of the Fathers*?
7 From whose point of view is the story told?
8 Would you say Trevor is a *round* character or a *flat* character?
9 In what way is there *irony* in the story?
10 Consider the patterns or construction of the sentences in this story (the *style* used by the writer) and compare the style here with the style in *Alleluia Morning* or *Millicent*. Is there any difference that you can notice?
11 Would you like to be able to write a story in a style like *The Sins of the Fathers*? Why, or why not?

C *The use of words*

1 Here are some words used in the story which you would find very useful at some time or other in writing or telling a story. Practise using them in oral sentences of your own.

swishing (1.9)   *whine* (1.11)   *draped* (1.68)   *speckling* (1.92)
crouched (1.94)   *swayed* (1.99)   *looped* (1.103)   *glinted* (1.105)
raked (1.109)
clutching (1.124)   *slim* (1.194)   *struggling* (1.00)

2   Discuss which word in each row is *nearest* in meaning to the one that is first and in italics.

seldom (1.16)   few   promptly   rarely   foolish
survive (1.17)   last   recover   develop   win
preserve (1.18)   finish   precede   rack   care
numerous (1.20)   metric   plentiful   confusing   numbered
dreaded (1.36)   long   smoked   feared   plaited
considered (1.44)   thought   fooled   decided   expressed
recognised (1.47)   counted   known   introduced   welcome
vision (1.59)   spirit   sight   mask   vengeance
paling (1.75)   pining   weakening   fence   whitening
range (1.59)   roam   reach   farm   wring

Beaming out

You might wish to work on one of these, or something else, in your spare time this week.

1   Pretend to be Trevor's father. Narrate how you felt about not being able to provide a turkey for your family for Easter, how you thought about it, what you did, and what happened afterwards.

Do not write *summary* more than is necessary. Write *scene* as much as possible.

2   Read the part of the story where Trevor is looking at the kites flying. Then, if you ever had a kite, try to remember a day when you flew one and describe all that happened, especially while the kite was in the air, remembering the pleasure and excitement you enjoyed and trying to put that into your story.

3   Imagine a person who wanted to give a birthday or Christmas present to someone who was very dear to him or her (like a grandson, son, daughter, wife or husband), but did not have the money to buy anything. Think of something which he or she decided to do to get some money and of some danger to be faced. Picture the events in your mind as clearly as you can and then write the story of what happened.

7 THE VALLEY OF COCOA
Michael Anthony

Tuning in

Far away places and big towns often seem more exciting and glamour-ous to some people than the familiar places they see every day. And West Indians nearly always think other countries are better than theirs. Perhaps what happened to the boy in this story should happen to all of us. Read it and see if you agree.

(*Cocoa* here means cacao, the fruit from which cocoa is made.)

There was not much in the valley of cocoa. Just the estate and our drying-houses, and our living-house. And the wriggling little river that passed through.

And of course, the labourers. But they didn't ever seem to speak to
5 anyone. Always they worked silently from sunrise to evening. Only Wills was different. He was friendly, and he knew lots of other things besides things about cocoa and drying-houses.

And he knew Port of Spain. He knew it inside out, he said. Every day after work he would sit down on the log with me and would tell of
10 the wonderful place.

As he spoke his eyes would glow with longing. The longing to be in that world which he said was part of him. And sometimes I knew pain. For Wills had made the city grow in me, and I knew longing too.

Never had I been out of the valley of cocoa. Father was only
15 concerned about his plantation, and nothing else. He was dedicated to wealth and prosperity, and every year the cocoa yielded more and more. So he grew busier and busier, building, experimenting, plan-ning for record returns. Everything needed out of the valley was handled by Wills—for people who knew Port of Spain could handle
20 anything. Business progressed. The valley grew greener with cocoa, and the drying-houses were so full that the woodmen were always felling timber to build more.

Wills, who one day had just returned from ordering new machinery in Port of Spain, sat talking with me. The sun had not long gone down
25 but already it was dusk. Wills said it was never so in Port of Spain. Port of Spain was always bright. He said as soon as the sun went down the whole city was lit by electric lamps, and you could hardly tell the difference between night and day.

And explained all about those lamps which he said hung from poles,
30 and from the houses that lined the million streets.

It was thick night when we got up. In the darkness Wills walked
straight on to a tree, and he swore, and said, By Jove—if that could
have happened to him in Port of Spain. He said one of these days I'd go
35 there, when I got big, and I'd see for myself, and I'd never want to
come back to the valley again.

The machinery arrived soon afterwards. It came in a shining new
van, and the name of the company was spelt in large letters on the sides
of the van. The driver was a bright gay-looking man and when the van
40 stopped he jumped out and laughed and called, 'Hey, there.'

Wills and Father went down to meet him and I eased up behind
them. I was thrilled. It was not every day that strangers came to the
valley.

Father looked worried as he spoke to the man about payments and
45 he complained that business wasn't doing well and the machinery was
so expensive. But the man was laughing all the time, and said who
cared about payments when Father had all the time in the world to
pay. Father was puzzled, and the man said, yes, Father could pay
instalments. Wills said it's true, that's what they did in Port of Spain.
50 The man made Father sign up for instalments and while Father signed,
the man pulled at my chin and said, 'Hi!'

Father was paying the first instalment. The man stretched his hands
for the money and without counting it put it into his pocket. Every
time my eyes caught his he winked.

55 'Hi!' he said softly.

I twined round Father's legs.

'Bashful,' he said, 'bashful,' and he tugged at the seat of my pants. I
couldn't help laughing.

He opened the door of the van and the next moment he was beside
60 me. He was smiling and dangling a bright-coloured packet. I held on
to Father's legs. Then I felt something slide into my pocket. I looked
up. 'Like sweets?' the man said. I turned away and grinned.

From about my father's legs I watched him. He pulled out a red
packet of cigarettes marked CAMEL on top. He passed the cigarettes to
65 Father, then to Wills, and as he lit theirs and lit himself one, he seemed
to be taken up with the estate below.

'All yours?' he asked after a while.

Father nodded.

He shook his head appraisingly. 'Nice—nice, old man!'

70 The evening was beginning to darken and the man looked at his
watch and said it was getting late and he's better start burning the gas.
Father said true, because Port of Spain was so far, and the country
roads were bad enough. The man claimed there were worse roads in

some parts of Port of Spain. And he laughed and said what's a van anyway, only a lot of old iron. Father and Wills laughed heartily at this, and the man turned a silver key and started the van. And he said, well, cheerio, cheerio, and if anything went wrong with the machine he'd hear from us.

The days that followed were filled with dream. I continually saw the gay city, and the bright laughing man. Port of Spain, I kept thinking. Port of Spain! I imagined myself among the tall red houses, the maze of streets, the bright cars and the vans darting to and fro; the trams, the trains, the buses; the thousands of people everywhere. And always I heard the voice. 'Hi!'—it kept sailing back to me. And every time I heard it I smiled.

Months passed, and more and more I grew fed up with the valley. I felt a certain resentment growing inside me. Resentment for everything around. For Father, for the silly labourers; even for Wills. For the cocoa trees. For the hills that imprisoned me night and day. I grew sullen and sick and miserable, tired of it all. I even wished for Father's fears to come true. *Witchbroom!* I wished witchbroom would come and destroy the cocoa and so chase Father from this dreary place.

As expected, the machinery soon went wrong. It wouldn't work. Wills had to rush to Port of Spain to get the man.

I waited anxiously towards the end of that evening, and when in the dusk I saw the van speeding between the trees I nearly jumped for sheer gladness.

From the hill Father shouted saying he didn't know what was wrong but the machine wouldn't start. The man said all right and he boyishly ran up the hill to the house. He stopped and played with me and I twined round Father's legs, and he tickled me and we both laughed aloud. Then he gave me sweets in a blue and white packet, and he said he'd better go and see to the machine because the machine was lazy and didn't want to work. He tried to tickle me again and I jumped away and we laughed, and Father and Wills and he went to the shed. They had not been there five minutes when I heard the machine start again.

The labourers had changed a little. They had become somewhat fascinated by the new machine. It seemed they sometimes stole chances to operate it, for the machine went wrong quite a number of times afterwards. And so, happily, the man often came to us.

In time Father and he became great friends. He gave Father all the hints about cocoa prices in the city and about when to sell and whom to sell to. He knew all the good dealers and all the scamps, he said.

He knew all the latest measures taken to fight cocoa diseases and he told Father what they did in West Africa, and what they did here and what they did there, to fight this, that and the other disease.

53

With his help Father did better than ever. And was so pleased that he
asked the man to spend a Sunday with us.

'Sure!' the man agreed. And I had run out then, and made two
happy somersaults on the grass.

That Sunday when the man arrived I was down the other side of the
hill grazing the goats. The voice had boomed down towards me.

'Kenneth!'

I turned and looked round. Then I dropped the ropes and ran
excitedly up the hill. 'Coming!' I kept saying. 'Coming!' When I got
there the big arms swept me up and threw me up in the air and caught
me.

Directly Father called us in to breakfast and afterwards the man put
shorts on and we went out into the fresh air. The whole valley of cocoa
nestled in the distance below us. The man watched like one under a
spell.

'Beautiful!' he whispered, shaking his head. 'Beautiful!'

'And the river,' I said. Strange! I had hardly noticed how pretty the
river was.

'Yes,' the man answered. 'Yellow, eh?'

I grinned.

'The water good?'

'Yes,' I said.

'Sure, sure?'

'Sure, sure,' I said.

'Well, come on?!' He took me by the hand and we hastened into the
house.

The next moment we were running down the hill towards the river,
the man in bathing trunks and me with my pants in my hand and sun
all over me. We reached the banks and I showed where was shallow
and where deep, and the man plunged into the deep part. He came to
the surface again, laughing and saying how nice the water was and
there was no such river in Port of Spain. He told me to get on his back,
and he swam upstream and down with me and then he put me to stand
in the shallow part. Then he soaped my body and bathed me, and
when I was rinsed we went and sat a little on the bank.

He sat looking around at the trees and up at the hill. I looked too at
the view. The cocoa seemed greener than I ever remembered seeing
them, and the immortelles which stood between them, for shade,
were like great giants, their blooms reddening the sky.

I looked up at him. We smiled.

Quietly then he talked of the city. He told me the city was lovely
too, but in a different way. Not like it was here. He said I must see the
city one of these days. Everything there was busy, he said. The cars
and buses flashed by, and people hurried into the shops, and out of the
shops, stores, hotels, hospitals, post offices, schools—everything.

Everything that made life easy. But sometimes he grew tired, he said,
165 of the hustle and bustle and nowhere to turn for peace. He said he liked
it here, quiet and nice. As life was meant to be. Then his eyes
wandered off to the green cocoa again, and the immortelles, and here
at the river, and up again to our house on the hill.

And he smiled sadly and said that he wished he was Father to be
170 living here.

We went back into the water for some time, then we finished, then
the man dried my skin, and we went up to the house.

After we had eaten Father took us into the cocoa field.

It was quiet there between the trees, and the dried brown leaves
175 underfoot, together with the ripening cocoa, put a healthy fragrance
in the air.

It was strange being so near those trees. Before I had only known
they were there and had watched them from the house. But now I was
right in the middle of them, and touching them.

180 We passed under immortelle trees with the ground beneath red with
dropped flowers and the man picked the loveliest of the flowers and
gave them to me. Father broke a cocoa pod, and we sucked the seeds
and juicy pulp, and really, the young cocoa was as sweet as Wills had
told me. The man sucked his seeds dry and looked as if he wanted
185 more, so I laughed. And Father watched from the corner of his eyes,
and knew, and he said, 'Let's look for a nice ripe cocoa.'

And it was already evening when we took the path out. Father and
the young man were talking and I heard Father ask him what he
thought of the place.

190 'Great, Mr Browne,' he had answered. 'Mr Browne, it's great, I'm
telling you!'

Late, late that night I eased up from my bed. I unlatched the window
and quietly shifted the curtain from one side.

The valley lay quietly below. The cocoa leaves seemed to be playing
195 with the moonlight, and the immortelles stood there, looking tall and
lonely and rapt in peace. From the shadows the moonlight spread
right across the river and up the hill.

'Beautiful . . . !' the voice sailed back to my mind. And I wondered
where he was now, if he was already in Port of Spain. He was sorry to
200 leave. He had said this was one of the happiest days he had known. I
had heard him telling Father how he liked the valley so much, and he
liked the little boy. I had cried, then.

And now it swept back to mind—what he had told Father just as he
was leaving. He had said, 'Mr Browne, don't be afraid for witch-
205 broom. Not a thing will happen. Just you use that spray—you
know—and everything will be all right.'

Quickly then I drew the curtains and latched the window. And I
squeezed the pillow to me, for joy.

Talking about it

A *The events of the story*

1 What was the name of the little boy in the story?
2 How did the boy's father earn his living?
3 What did Wills get the boy to feel and think about Port of Spain?
4 What business did the man have with the boy's father?
5 How did the man show his liking for the little boy?
6 How did the little boy get to feel about the man?
7 How did the man show what he thought about the valley of Cocoa?
8 *And I squeezed the pillow to me, for joy* (l.207). What was he feeling joy about?

B *The writing skills*

1 Which of these does the writer want to tell us about?
   a) how a man and a little boy became friends
   b) how a cocoa estate was saved from witchbroom disease
   c) how a boy learnt to love his home
   d) how towns can be bad places
2 Here is an outline or plan of the story which the author might have had in his mind before writing the story.

   Boy feels fed up with home surroundings. Yearns for bright life of Port of Spain. Man from Port of Spain comes to sell machinery. Shows friendliness to boy. Returns many times to repair machinery. Boy becomes fond of him. Man shows how he yearns for quiet life of the valley. Boy becomes happy about home surroundings.

   Notice how bare and empty this plan or outline is when compared with the story itself. What did Michael Anthony do to make the story come to us as if we were seeing it in real life?
3 Are the sentences used by the writer (the *style*) difficult to understand or easy to understand?
4 Could this story have been written by a boy or girl at school?
5 From whose *point of view*, or from inside of whom, is the story told?
6 What is *ironic* about the different ways the boy and the man felt about Port of Spain and the cacao estate?
7 How much do you know about the boy or the man? Is either one of them a *round* character?
8 'The boy in the story is a *symbol* used to represent or stand for other people.' Do you agree or disagree?

9   Do you think the story is a sentimental one, with the writer exaggerating the feelings of the boy and the man, or not?

C   *The use of words*

1   The words below, used in *The Valley of Cocoa,* are useful for describing things around us. If you look at how each one is used in the story you will get a good idea of how to use it, if you did not know before. When you think you can, use them in oral sentences of your own.

wriggling (1.2)   *glow* (1.11)   *maze* (1.82)   *darting* (1.83)
sullen (1.91)   *dreary* (1.93)   *anxiously* (1.96)   *sheer* (1.98)
fascinated (1.110)   *boomed* (1.124)   *excitedly* (1.127)   *nestled* (1.132)
hastened (1.143)   *bustle* (1.165)   *fragrance* (1.175)   *rapt* (1.196)

2   See if you can write five sentences, using two of these words in each one:

concerned (1.15)   *dedicated* (1.15)   *prosperity* (1.16)   *yielded* (1.16)
resentment (1.88)   *surface* (1.149)   *wandered* (1.167)   *shifted* (1.193)

Beaming out

You might find one of these interesting to do in your spare time this week. Keep it in your folder for group or private discussion, if you wish.

1   Try to use this outline to write a story that makes readers see it as if it is happening in real life.

Girl thinks parents are old-fashioned and too strict. Wishes her friend's parents were her parents. Friend comes to spend a few days with her. Friend praises girl's parents and wishes they were hers. Girl feels happy with her parents now.

2   See if you can remember an occasion when some friendly visitor came to your home or school when you were much younger. Relate what you noticed, what happened, what you did, and so on, as if you were still at that age.

3   Imagine you were Kenneth in *The Valley of Cocoa,* and that you did get a chance to spend a day or two in a town, where some unpleasant experiences make you think how much better you would enjoy being back at home.
    Write the story of your time in the town, in the form of a letter to a friend.

8 SEPTIMUS
John Wickham

Tuning in

Perhaps you would know that it is not always easy to get what you want if you have several brothers and sisters to get things too. But it hurts sometimes, doesn't it? Here we see how Septimus took it.
(*Filial* (1.13) = like a dutiful son or daughter; *to yodel* = to do a special kind of singing; *a decanter* = a vessel of decorated glass in which liquor is poured or kept; *a hope-chest* = a collection of things a woman makes with the hope that she will get married one day.)

———

Mama is in tears with the letter in her hand, and I know that she has heard from Seppy. Mama always cries when she hears from Seppy, but at Christmas her tears have a special meaning. Mama's tears are now, and have been long before Seppy ever went to Canada,
5 a part of our family's Christmas rites.

For Mama there is no such person as Seppy. Our little brother, the last of us, may be Seppy for us, his sisters, but for Mama he has always been Septimus. 'Your father,' she has always insisted, 'called him Septimus because he was the seventh, and that is his name.' And so for
10 the sake of the Season, the six of us girls make a point of saying Septimus, just to please the old girl.

She is in tears. I take the letter from her hand and read it. Septimus has sent a 'little something' for her, but it is not this act of filial thoughtfulness that makes Mama cry. It is the last sentence of Seppy's
15 Christmas letter: 'Tell the girls that at last I can have a whole apple for Xmas.' When I remember the origin of that sentence, I feel a little like crying too.

We have always lived in the Gap—a narrow lane between the canefields, just a little longer than a cricket pitch, although it seemed a
20 boundless highway to us at the time I am now remembering. There were three houses in the Gap at this time, one belonging to old Bostic, the watchmaker, our own, and, at the far end, right on the edge of the canes, a ramshackle old gabled house, smelling of mice, mildew, and camphor, where Aunt Bless lived.

25 The seven of us ruled the Gap. We shall never, however rich we may become, ever possess anything as completely as we possessed the Gap.

It was ours from the stones and potholes, to the trees in each backyard, from old Bostic, grumpy, pulling his moustache, to old 30 Bostic's cow, Blossom, which he put out to graze every morning before he left for his little shop in Bridgetown.

I don't think old Bostic really liked children, but there was nothing he could do about our ownership of him: he used to put up with us and make the best of it. Sometimes he would even play his guitar for us, 35 and, if he had a few drinks, he might even go so far as to yodel—a magnetic performance which made him seem wonderfully different from the tightly-wrapped-up lonely old self.

Aunt Bless was a willing, even eager, possession of ours. Her fruit trees, her garden, all the strange things in her front room—she had a 40 what-not, an epergne, a cut-glass decanter full of camphor-water, and a collection of turban-like hats like those worn by old Queen Mary—all of them belonged to us.

Even her name belonged to us, for it was Septimus who christened her Aunt Bless. Before he was born we used to call her Aunt Letty (her 45 name was Letitia), but as soon as he could speak he called her Aunt Bless. Septimus was the first of us to notice that she never used the conventional greetings of 'Good morning' or 'Good evening'. It was always 'Bless you, Maisie' (to Mama) or 'Bless you child', to one of us. Needless to say, Septimus was her favourite.

50 One Christmas Eve when the six of us girls were ready to go along to Aunt Bless with the basket of cake and ginger beer which Mama made for her every Christmas, Septimus, who must have been six or so at the time, did not want to go. He was in a bad mood.

Mama had not long before come back from town with her bag full 55 of sweets and presents she had bought for us. There were packages of peppermints wrapped in shiny red paper, oranges, a tiny motor-car for Septimus, hair ribbons for us girls in pink and yellow and blue, a big picture book for all of us, and three apples, red and rosy on the top of the bag.

60 Immediately he saw the apples, Septimus grabbed one of them and ran off. We all ran behind him and caught him under the breadfruit tree at the back of the house before he had time to do more than fondle the rich redness of the apple.

We dragged him back to the house howling and kicking. Mama 65 gave him a lecture: 'No, Septimus,' she scolded, 'there are only three apples, and we must share them among all nine of us.' We all knew that our father would give Septimus his share, but the principle had to be established that what we had—which was not much—had none the less to be shared among all nine of us.

'I want a whole apple,' Septimus shouted in protest, too young to understand.

'You can't have a whole one,' Mama said, 'and that's that.' When Mama spoke, she spoke.

'And now,' she said, drying his tears with her handkerchief, 'You just stop crying and go with the girls up to Aunt Bless to take her her Christmas.'

Aunt Bless greeted us and hugged all seven of us, one after the other, overpowering us with the scent of Khus-khus root with which she perfumed her clothes, and murmuring 'Bless you, child,' with each embrace. She took the basket from Maria, the eldest (very ladylike on these occasions—'playing Mama') who had a protective arm around Septimus who was still snivelling.

'What's wrong?' Aunt Bless asked, concerned that her darling boy was not happy. 'What's wrong, Septimus? Tomorrow is Christmas!'

Septimus did not answer. He just stood there, fighting back the tears and looking foolish. But his feelings were too much for him and he blurted out between his sobs: 'I want a whole apple and Mama says No?'

Aunt Bless grasped the situation right away. She gathered Septimus to her, her own eyes now swimming with love and feeling, and she hugged him and kissed him and told him not to mind: that Aunt Bless would see that he got a whole apple, because he was her own little Septimus.

At last Septimus stopped crying, and Aunt Bless took him into her bedroom where it seemed to us children that not even the sun went, and then we heard sounds of rummaging and scuffling as if Aunt Bless were turning out all the treasures of her hope-chest. And then Septimus' laughter pealed out as clear and silver as a bell.

Septimus came out of the darkness of Aunt Bless's room with his eyes shining bright and as big as saucers and clutching in his hand the biggest rosiest apple I have ever seen.

All the way home Septimus held his apple to his bosom. He said not a word to any of us. I think we were a little ashamed of him and the scene we had made, and we knew that Mama would be angry with us for letting him accept the apple.

When we got home, Septimus ran to the kitchen and we hurried to tell Mama what had happened. All of us tried to talk at the same time, and it was not easy for Mama to get the story. But she did at last, and she was so angry that she did not speak.

She rushed out to the kitchen with all of us trooping behind her. But she was too slow, for Septimus met her at the kitchen-door with a saucer in his hand.

'Bless you, children,' he said, 'Bless you, children.' And he handed Mama the saucer with nine slices of apple on it.

Talking about it

A *The events of the story*

1 Who is the narrator in the story?
2 What caused the narrator to remember a certain Christmas Eve?
3 What always happened when Mama received a letter from Septimus?
4 Where was Septimus when he wrote the letter saying he could have a whole apple for Christmas?
5 What does the narrator mean by saying they *possessed the Gap* (1.26)?
6 Why was Septimus given that name, and how did Aunt Bless come to be called that?
7 What is meant by *the principle had to be established* (1.67)?
8 *Aunt Bless grasped the situation* (1.89). What do you understand by that?
9 What did Aunt Bless do to make Seppy happy that Christmas?
10 How did Seppy surprise his sisters and mother?

B *The writing skills*

1 Would you like to be able to write in the style used by the author in this story? *(The way he used language, or the way the sentences are expressed.)* If so, say why.
2 Did you notice that the writer began the story using the present tense: *Mama IS in tears,* and so on? Then, later, he wrote in the past tense: *He WAS in a bad mood,* and so on? Where does he change the narration from present tense to past tense? Do you think the writer had any kind of reason for beginning with the present tense and changing to the past tense?
3 What, would you guess, came into the author's mind, or what might have happened, to give him the idea for making up this story?
4 What are some of the little details the writer put in to make the story seem real, as if it is happening before you right now?
5 What do you think the author had in mind as the *theme* of the story: the general observation about life that he wanted to make?
6 Is there anything amusing in the story or the way it is told?

C *The use of words*

1 Look at the first word in each row below. If you observe how it is used in the story you can make a good guess about its meaning.

Discuss which word in the same row is nearest in meaning to it.

rites (l.5) feelings customs presents
origin (l.16) birth country basement
conventional (l.47) usual stale tremendous
protest (l.70) acceptance march disagreement
embrace (l.80) repel sever hug
snivelling (l.82) digging sobbing circling
blurted (l.87) avoided swollen blabbed
rummaging (l.96) howling doubting searching

2   Discuss which one of these words best fits into each sentence:

insisted (l.8)   *murmuring* (l.79)   *protective* (l.81)   *concerned* (l.83)
accept (l.105)

a)   They thought he was wrong to _____ the gift that was
       offered to him.
b)   Although he knew it was wrong he _____ on doing it.
c)   She was _____ to herself as she went along.
d)   The father put a _____ arm around his son.
e)   I was very _____ about what Mother would say.

Beaming out

If you try to write in the simple, straight forward way in which
Septimus was written you would be on the right track towards
becoming a good writer. Also, if you take simple experiences that you
are familiar with and use them to imagine stories of your own.

   You might like to use one of these ideas, or any other you prefer, to
write a story this week to be kept in your folder and to discuss with
your friends and teacher if you wish.

1   Think about Christmas and how your family celebrate it. Then try
      to imagine you were somebody else and that something happened
      about a present you were to receive, or did receive, one Christmas.
         In your mind, put some events together to form a story and,
      when you have an idea of how the story can go, think of a way to
      begin narrating it. Then begin to write it, but if you get new ideas
      as you go along feel free to use them.
2   Imagine you saw a family with five brothers and one sister, who is
      the youngest. Think about something that could happen one day
      when the sister and her brothers had a disagreement.
         Narrate the scene or scenes that you imagine with the little
      details that would make the story seem to be happening before the
      reader as he reads.

9 WHEN YOU WERE VERY YOUNG
Bernard C. Graham

Tuning in

Adults make the world a place where people are divided against other people, often for no good reason at all. And they teach children to judge people without knowing anything about them. They teach them prejudices.

In this story a sad loss is brought into a little boy's life by his mother for no good reason at all.

———

It's one of those humid afternoons in August, with everything seeming to droop from lack of life. Even the dogs slouch across the street, saliva running from their tongues like water from a tap. It's uncomfortable and irritating so that when you start any manual work,
5 you have to stop half-way. It's too hot to concentrate, what with physical strain drenching you with perspiration, like a sweat-vein was busted. So you're getting under your mother's skin in the house, till she yells at you and says, for Pete's sake, go outside and play! And you go outside and sit on top of the wall that runs alongside the house,
10 almost out to the street, and pelt stones at this sickly, white (well, it used to be white) dog that Miss Caro always threatens you with when you scamp mangoes from her tree. When the dog takes off, you find that there's this woman coming down the street and her face reminds you of the battle-axe you read about in the English History book. So
15 you start making faces at her and when she passes, you shout, 'Queen Canute!' and she says in this bass voice, the children of today! And she goes on down the street and you continue making these ugly faces at her back until you get tired.

Then you just sit on the wall and wait.
20 You fix your eyes up the street and you're waiting for him to come around the bend. You're watching the bend and wondering what he has for you today. And you start thinking of tamarind-balls and golden apples, and the thought increases your salivary output so you know that if you hang out your tongue, it'll drip like the dog's. You
25 don't have long to wait. Every afternoon, around this time, he comes around the bend, with his shuffling old-man's walk, wearing the same clothes that you first saw him in. The pants that were once grey, and now, from incessant wear, almost colourless, with patches at the seat. The jacket, once parson's-grey but now almost as colourless as the

pants. And the felt hat, which is stained all around the rim with dirt, from the many times he pulled it down over his eyes. You don't wait long.

The shuffling walk comes around the bend and you're glad. Your heart misses that beat as it always does when he rounds the bend. Immediately, you start to think that you get a whiff of a musty odour, associated with unwashed bodies, old-clothes and old-age. An odour, not too unbearable, but not like how your mother smells after she uses that flower-sweet, scented soap in the bathroom. But it's him—you welcome the scent. You watch him come closer and when he sees you, he squints and the wrinkles on his face multiply at a fantastic rate as he smiles, a wide smile that pulls the lips from his mouth and exposes that dark, mysterious opening where teeth were once planted. That smile is the signal and you start singing in your high-pitched voice:

'Adam in the garden hiding,
Hiding, hiding.
Adam in the garden hiding,
He hiding from the Lord.'

And he laughs, a cough-racked, rumbling, cold-filled laugh and continues the song in his cracking old-man's bass:

'Oh! Adam, where is Eve?
Adam, where is Eve?
Adam, where is Eve?
She hiding from the Lord.'

He reaches you by then, snatches you off the wall, throws you into the air, catches you, hugs you, puts you on the ground. And all the time, he is laughing and you are laughing, because this is your good, trusted friend—and you are his only ally.

He feels in the deep pockets of the old jacket and chants: 'Guess one, guess two, guess what I bring for you.'

You close your eyes and reply: 'Tamarind-balls and sugar-cake, or nice sweet bread that you just bake.'

He pulls out his hand and gives you two of the biggest, softest, dark-brown sugar-cakes you ever saw and you start eating.

You both climb on the wall and sit, looking out on the street. You, chewing your sugar-cake, and he, in his old-man's voice, talking with the words punctuated by the lack of teeth. You're chewing and looking out on the street, but you're hearing everything he says. 'Cause he is telling you about the time when all animals had horns. Dogs and cats and cows and horses and sheep and goats—they all had horns. And they used to work together, sleep together, eat together, play together. They were all a happy bunch. But one day, one of the dogs got into a fight and killed one of the cows with its horns. And from that day, the horns from all dogs and those animals which were on their side, dropped off. So that today, you find these animals

75 without horns are afraid to encounter those with horns.

Picture it. You—a boy of six—when the story is finished, puzzled by questions.

But why they lived together in the first place?

Why they all had to have horns?

80 So you mean that the same way you have dogs as pets, at one time cows and horses used to be pets and used to sleep in kennels?

He laughs and shakes his head, and looks in the distance, like he is looking far away where you can't see.

'Because that was the time when God meant everything to be one, 85 for everything to be equal. Men and dogs and cats and sheep and goats and horses and cows.'

And that makes you more puzzled so you ask him if it isn't so now. And he smiles.

'You're still young. But when you get big and go out and see for 90 yourself, then you'll know.'

But before you can ask anything more, he pulls you down from the wall and says it's time for your fighting lessons.

Ever since the time some boys from the Wharf beat you up, he teaches you to fight and defend yourself.

95 Down you go and he crouches and tells you to do the same, but balance yourself on both feet with weight evenly distributed. Lead with your left, keep the right tucked in for the Blow. You're coming along real good. This evening, he's pleased with how you're doing. And when he's pleased, you're delighted, because he's your good 100 friend and you're his only ally.

All that August, you and Adam are close. He tells you more stories, you learn to fight properly—and the amount of things he brings you! Every time he comes, there's something in those deep pockets for you. Those days are pleasant ones. For at that young age you realise 105 what a good thing it is to have a friend like Adam.

Then one evening, there's a change.

Your mother sees you eating something he brings for you and she yells at you and says, 'Don't take anything from that old man again, if I catch you—you can't realise you're not the same? You are different 110 to him! Don't let me see you near him again!'

You're puzzled, doubts harass you, questions—but you can't have them answered. Your mother is angry. These questions are never answered.

But there's a change. Now you run away and hide whenever you 115 see Adam approaching. But he'd come and stand by the wall and look around, waiting for you. But you don't go. You never go. And one evening, hiding from him, peeping through the window, you see him look up at the house. The wrinkles are long and sad on his face, but his face says, I understand now, it's okay, I understand. And he turns and

66

20 goes back down the street with his shuffling walk, and you never see
him again.

You sneak out from the house and watch the spot where he was
standing, waiting for you. And you want to cry. Your good
friend—but your mother told you. There's a difference between you.
25 You're not sure what it is, but you think you know there is a difference
between Old Man Adam and you.

But sometimes, at nights in particular, you still get a faint whiff of a
musty odour that reminds you of unwashed skins, old-clothes and
old-age. Sometimes, you think that at one time, dogs and cats and
30 cows and sheep and horses and goats all had horns. But they don't any
more.

But you're young and you soon forget.

Talking about it

A   The events of the story

1   *Then you sit on the wall and wait* (1.19). Who sits? To wait for what?
2   What do you think is meant by *a whiff of a musty odour* (1.35)?
3   What usually happened between the boy and Adam?
4   What tale or fable did Adam tell the boy?
5   What puzzled the boy about the fable Adam told him?
6   What was the meaning of the fable?
7   Before the mother said what she did about Adam, what told you
    of a difference in the lives of the boy and Adam?
8   How long did the friendship between the boy and Adam last?
9   What tells you how the boy felt about not being able to go to
    Adam any more?
10 How do you know how Adam felt about the boy not coming to
    talk with him any more?
11 Did the boy understand why his mother had that attitude towards
    Adam?
12 What did the boy learn about people from that episode?

B   The writing skills

1   Is the *style* of the sentences difficult and complicated or simple and
    straightforward?
2   What feeling or feelings does the writer make you have after
    reading the story?
3   Do you suppose the writer got the idea for making up this story
    because it happened to him, or because he knew about class
    prejudices, or because he saw it happen, or what?
4   Stories are usually told in the past tense, because they tell of

something that happened already. In *Septimus* the author began
with the present tense and then used the past tense. In *When You
Were Very Young* the writer used the present tense right through.
Did that make it hard for you to understand that the events were
past? Or did it help to make the story seem as if it were happening
right now before your eyes?

5 Why do you suppose the writer put in Adam's fable about when
everything was meant to be one and equal?

6 Do you think the problem or *conflict* of the story is between the boy
and his mother or between different feelings inside the boy?

7 According to what you think the *conflict* or problem is, say where
the *climax* of the story comes, the time when the problem is finally
decided one way or the other.

8 Which of these would you say is nearest to the *theme* of the story
that the writer was concerned with?

   a)   how people live in different ways
   b)   how children learn their parents' prejudices
   c)   how people are unkind to children

C   *The use of words*

Most of the words in this story are used in such a way that you can
figure out their meanings if you did not know them before. For
instance, you can tell that *ally* (1.57) means friend, from the way it is
used.

1 Look back at how each one of these is used and then try to use each
one in oral sentence:

   humid (1.1)   *slouch* (1.2)   *whiff* (1.35)   *odour* (1.35)   *chants* (1.58)
   crouches (1.95)   *delighted* (1.99)   *sneak* (1.122)

2 Pair off each word in list A with its partner in list B:

   A   *irritating* (1.4)   *incessant* (1.28)   *associated* (1.36)
       exposes (1.41)   *encounter* (1.75)   *harass* (1.111)

   B   ceaseless   bother   shows   meet   joined   annoying

3 Discuss which one of these words best fits into each of the
sentences below:

   drenching (1.6)   *threatens* (1.11)   *squints* (1.40)   *fantastic* (1.40)
   rumbling (1.48)   *distributed* (1.96)

   a)   It was _____ how his face changed when he smiled.
   b)   Soon after he arrives you will hear the _____ of his laughter.
   c)   The rain came down suddenly, _____ me to the skin.

d) He looks at you but _____ to try to see you better.
e) She _____ him with punishment if he associates with that person.
f) In a good community the benefits are _____ equally to rich and poor.

Beaming out

1 Do you remember seeing or being in any incident when someone was forbidden to associate with someone else? If you do, try to recall all that you can about the persons concerned and all that happened when the warning was given, all that happened before, and what happened afterwards.

Then use those ideas (or imagine others like them) to make up a story which you can narrate in the present tense or the past tense, as you wish.

2 Write this as the opening of a story:

It is one of those cool, star-filled nights when everything gives you the feeling of being quiet and peaceful. You sit on . . .

Then think of how you can continue the events of the night. First, think of a difficulty or question that might come up between two people or between different feelings in the same person. Then think about what leads up to it, how it will be decided, and so on.

When you have imagined a few things that might happen continue writing the story in the present tense as you began.

3 Adam in *When You Were Very Young* and Aunt Bless in *Septimus* both had smells that the children noticed.

Try to make up a person who has a certain kind of pleasant smell and relate an incident that took place one day between that person and a child or children.

4 Make up a story to bring out one of these as its theme:

a) old people sometimes have better relationships with children than parents;
b) people do not always keep their promises;
c) a child can be deeply hurt by someone's careless remark;
d) prejudices cause unhappiness.

10 LANDSLIDE WEATHER
Cecil Gray

Tuning in

Have you ever wondered about a person you have seen begging alms, and thought about how he or she became a beggar? In this story a man's pride made him prefer to fight his own battles and not beg anybody for anything. Did he win?

(A *ravine* is a gully; *kith* and *kin* are family and friends; *bonafide* means lawful.)

———

When the rain began falling that year, and the roads became pock-marked with muddy craters, Manuel remembered the crumbling edge of the ravine and how last year two feet of earth had been sucked down by the greedy stream suddenly getting its fill. The
5 hills were a vivid green, too rich for the eye, as if after the long brown months they had drunk too much of the July rains and now were bursting with excessive life.

Manuel was glad now that the rains had come. The corn would shoot high and the bananas would take on maturity. There would be
10 grass and bush for the goats and he would not have to go far to tie them out. It was a busy time. It was time for many weedings, time for moulding, time for transplanting and hoeing, and perhaps to service the two young goats he bought last year from Mr Valdez across the valley. He did not think it necessary to worry about the ravine eating
15 away his land, first because it was not really his land, and secondly because he did not mistrust the ravine. It had never done him any real harm.

People it was who had done him harm, Manuel would say. And he would say too it was because of people that he was now alone, an old
20 man, without friends, without contact with kith or kin, fighting his own battle, proud. His body was strong for his age and his eyes undimmed, so he did not regret the strange life he led, all by himself in his little ajoupa up the side of the mountain. He remained in his lonely world and had no wish to venture out of it. From his doorway he
25 could see all the way across the plain and the shimmering Gulf.

It was many years Manuel had not gone down the valley to the plain, many years he had not gone to Port of Spain on the edge of the Gulf. He had no need. Sometimes, as he sat under the stars with his pipe looking over the constellations of lights scattered far below, he
30 would wish to go to Port of Spain again, to see what it was like now, what was different, and new. But he never did.

There was a shop down in the village, Aripo, and there he bought such things as flour and salt and cooking oil. He sold the milk of the goats and with the money did business in the shop. Some of it he saved
35 in a little box that he kept under a big stone near his door. Sometimes he would bring down produce from the soil and he would sit under the shop and wait for someone to approach him. He would never call anyone to buy for he was too proud and did not want to seek a favour of anyone. The people in the village all called him 'stuck up' and selfish
40 and as he passed in the road, often he would hear the children cry 'Manuel the Great' in echo of their parents.

It was a long time ago that Manuel had come through the village for the first time. He was a young man then but already he had no sweetness left in him. His heart was bitter inside him. That was why
45 he had come to poach on the Marlay lands. Marlay, Manuel had said, had made him a pauper, had cheated and robbed him and broken his spirit, so that it was only fair to retrieve from his land a quota of recompense. And in all that time Marlay had never ejected him.

Each year he had spread his garden to cover a little more ground,
50 clearing away the bushes and rooting out the stumps that clung so tenaciously to the soil, until at last he came up against the ravine. Then the ravine had begun slyly sucking away the ground, sometimes in tiny bits, sometimes in gulps, reclaiming from Manuel some of the wrested territory. Manuel enjoyed the humour of the situation,
55 promising himself each year next time to put bamboo to bank the crumbling earth.

And now another rainy season had come. Manuel shrugged his shoulders and went about his work. It did not matter if the ravine swallowed pieces of the land. It would be the last time. And next year
60 he would stretch his furrows on the other side and higher up the slope. For many days the clouds brought silver rain and drenched the parched earth. The soil turned black and rivulets began to push impermanent paths out of the loose top soil. Then, when all the water had drained out of the sky, the sun shone hot and bright for several
65 days. It was a breathing space for which Manuel was thankful and the old man hummed cheerfully as his wearying limbs did their chores.

The morning that rain began falling again the sky was dressed in ash. Many hours passed and still the water poured. Torrents tore through the air and splayed the mountainside into a myriad shallow
70 fissures. The rivulets joined and washed over the ground, clearing its face of pimply pebbles, and later of rocks and stones. Manuel could not remember the year it rained like that. It would mean much more work reshaping beds, rescuing damaged plants. He stood at the back of his shack and looked up at the sheets of water coming down. And it
75 was while he was doing that that gently, tentatively, the earth moved beneath him.

He stiffened. He wanted to think he had imagined it, that it was his fancy playing him tricks and there was no shudder. He stood there frightened, without moving, wildly looking about him. And the earth moved again, then he saw. The ravine was a ravine no longer. The land was letting go of its moorings, rapidly surrendering itself into the ravine and making of it a widening gorge. Manuel stood petrified, waiting for the disintegration under his feet, and through the turmoil of his panic an image of the money he had saved in the little box under the stone rushed by. Swiftly he moved through the ajoupa and his frantic fingers quickly dislodged the stone. And as he grasped the box everything around him jolted and shifted, throwing him to the ground.

The ajoupa suddenly turned askew and cracked up before his eyes and Manuel felt himself drawn down into the mud and the slush, clawing hopelessly for a hold in the amorphous mass. He was faintly aware of rocks that struck him about the face and shoulders and horned branches that tore and tugged at him. Then he knew nothing else.

After the rain there was much stir in the village. The villagers indulged themselves in a flutter of excitement, pressing every vestige of drama from the unusual happenings. Talk of the rain and of the landslide made voices run in hour-long babel at the corner near the shop. Heads wagged and fingers punctuated the garrulous flow of repetitive chatter. No one remembered Manuel, until a little boy came up and said he had looked up the hill for Manuel's house and it wasn't there.

They found him later that day under a mound of debris that had almost covered him. His forehead bled and he was unconscious. When his legs were free and they could lift him they carried him slowly down the slope to the village. They put him on Thompson the fisherman's truck after the fish were taken out and somebody said to take him to the St Joseph hospital.

The journey was rough over the stony road but Manuel did not become conscious until it ended. The nurse at the hospital listened to the two men who had brought him in and Manuel groaned as she passed her hands over his aching body. 'Lucky,' she said. 'No fractures. Only a few cuts and bruises. We'll keep him a few days I suppose.' The men thanked her, gave the name of the village again, and clambered back aboard the truck.

For three long quiet days Manuel remained at the hospital. Most of the time he thought of his ajoupa and the land that was no longer there. Every time he tried to look into the future he couldn't think what to think about, until he gave up trying and decided to talk to one of the nurses about his troubles. He waited patiently that night, pretending to be asleep. When he saw the night nurse getting restless he knew that

that was the best time to go to her because it was then she wanted company, or something to occupy her, to keep her from falling asleep. He went up to the little table in the middle of the room.

125 'Nurse,' he said, 'I want to ask you something.'

'What is it?' she said, in a detached professional manner.

'I have nowhere to go now, Nurse,' Manuel said. 'I don't know what to do. I want somebody to tell me something.'

The night nurse, a short, plump, efficient woman, looked hard at
130 Manuel, a shade of puzzlement on her face.

'Is hard for me to ask anybody to help me, Nurse,' he went on haltingly. 'For years uh force mihself to do without people help. But now, well, uh feel so alone. I don' think I could go back and start all over again. Uh too old to build ajoupa. I en' got the heart, or the
135 strength. An' uh en' got no money. Not a cent.' He paused. Then he added, 'What to do? Nurse, what to do?'

The nurse did not yet understand and Manuel had to tell her everything. In the end she did not have anything to tell Manuel. She wanted to help, she said, but she did not know what to say. Manuel
140 thanked her and walked through the dim sleeping ward with the throbbing of the clock loud in his ear. He lay back on his pillow, his palms behind his head, but it was nearly dawn when he fell into a doze.

That day he was to be discharged from the hospital. The doctor told him he was a lucky old man, but he should have somebody to live with
145 him. He asked Manuel if he had any money to get home and when Manuel said no, he took a shilling out of his pocket and gave it to him. Manuel did not want to take it but before he knew it he stammered his thanks, said he would pay it back, and went to say goodbye to the nurse. The day nurse gave him a shake by the shoulder saying how
150 better he was and then shook his hand and watched him make his way to the door.

When he was reaching for the step she called out to him . . .

'I forgot to tell you,' she said when she came up, 'I read something in the papers this morning about the landslide and the people in the
155 village who had losses by it. The papers say you all going to get some relief, so you coming in for some raise, Manuel.' She smiled broadly. Manuel's heart grew large within him and he could feel it pressing against his chest. This was hope at last. A light.

'Where Nurse?' he asked. 'Where they giving it?'

160 'I think you have to go the the Red House, to the Minister of something or the other,' the nurse said. 'Anyhow ask somebody in the Red House. They will tell you where to go.'

She turned away before Manuel could say anything more, but his tread was firmer now as he walked through the gate, and his thoughts
165 clearer. He would take a bus and he would travel to Port of Spain. Somebody would tell him how to find the Red House, because he had

forgotten where it was. And there he would find out about the relief, the relief, thank God.

People in the city did not laugh at him when he asked them questions but to Manuel it seemed they looked at him strangely and he was never sure if he should follow what they said. He had travelled on the bus and he had walked many streets seeing so many people and cars and things he did not quite understand. At the Red House they were kind to him. They all directed him with kindly tolerant smiles. Finally he was sent to a woman at a desk in a tidy room at the end of the building. She was somebody's secretary they made him understand.

He went in and stood a little distance in front of the wide desk. She took a long time before she looked up and asked him what he wanted. Manuel felt like running back out. His explanation tumbled out of him in disconnected slabs and he could see the woman was getting impatient. When he was finished she asked him his name and then said, 'All right, sit outside. I'll see about you in a while.'

Manuel sat on the bench outside for a long, long time, watching people go and come, watching the traffic and the meaningless bustle. He was hungry but he had spent the shilling the doctor gave him and he would ask of no one. He would wait until the relief came he determined, however long they kept him. He was falling asleep when the woman came to the door and called him in. He got up shakily and followed her. She sat down and made him sit down too in a chair near the desk. Then she began to tell him.

She had a report on file she said. She had the names of all the villagers who were entitled to relief. Manuel's was not among them. The investigator had written something about Manuel yes, but it was not for relief she said. In the first place Manuel was not a bonafide tenant. He was a trespasser. The woman waited a little for Manuel to say something. He had his head bowed but he did not speak. The woman went on. The report blamed Manuel for the landslide, she said. It said he had cleared the side of the mountain near the ravine and removed the roots that held the soil together. As the soil was loosened by his depredations, the report said, in that area a landslide was inevitable. She was sorry she said, but she was afraid she could do nothing to help.

Outside, the traffic noises grew more numerous and louder as offices disgorged typists and clerks, principal officers and messengers. Manuel fumbled out into the afternoon sunlight. He walked through the Square under the cool trees and passed vacantly by the fountain, his mind empty and afraid. When he reached the opposite gate he stood up without knowing why, without knowing where he was going, and, slowly, thought came back to him. He was a lost speck of dust, spinning in space.

He leaned against the iron railing, heedless of the hurrying people brushing by. It seemed a long time ago, in another world, he was living in a little ajoupa above the village Aripo looking down over the plain. A little distance away he saw a ragged man, his palm held out, 215 begging alms. And higher up the street another. Leaning against the iron railing.

Manuel rested his head back on the spike, feeling himself crumble into rags and bones. His pride petered out of him and as he closed his eyes he could feel his manhood ooze out of his body and into the earth. 220 When he opened his eyes again a well-dressed young man was approaching. As he drew near Manuel said, his voice choking a little in his throat, 'Mister . . . gimme a penny please,' and held his palm out before him.

The man passed on.

Talking about it

A *The events of the story*

1 Where did Manuel live?
2 What made him go to live there?
3 What did he do in that place?
4 Why did the people of the village call him 'Manuel the Great?'
5 *Each year he had spread his garden to cover a little more ground, clearing away the bushes and rooting out the stumps* (1.49). What did that cause to happen?
6 What did Manuel try to save when the landslide was taking place?
7 How did he come to be found afterwards?
8 Where was he taken when he was found?
9 What worried him while he was in the hospital?
10 Why did he go to the Red House?
11 What did the woman in the Red House tell him?
12 What did he find himself doing like the others near the railing of the Square?

B *The writing skills*

1 Apart from what happened up the mountainside, what else do you think the title of the story refers to?
2 What connection is made in the *plot* of the story between Manuel's actions and his having to become a beggar?
3 Would you agree that Manuel's character was the cause of everything that happened?
4 How do you suppose the writer got the idea to imagine this story?

5   Do you think the story has a *theme*: something the writer had in
    mind about real life? Is it any one of these?

    a)   how thoughtlessness causes trouble
    b)   the loss of manhood
    c)   the cruelty of governments

6   Can you think of any reason why the *point of view* in the story is
    that of an eye outside the story?

7   The nurses and doctor said Manuel was lucky. Do you think there
    is *irony* in that or not?

8   These words are used *metaphorically* in the story: *drunk* (1.6),
    constellations (1.29), *echo* (1.41), *sweetness* (1.44). Can you find four or
    five other words used in the same way?

C   *The use of words*

1   Study the *context* in which each of these words is used in the story
    and try to use it in an oral sentence of your own.

    vivid (1.5)   *shimmering* (1.25)   *drenched* (1.61)   *parched* (1.62)
    torrents (1.68)   *shudder* (1.78)   *panic* (1.84)   *frantic* (1.86)
    jolted (1.87)   *clawing* (1.91)   *throbbing* (1.141)   *crumble* (1.217)

2   According to how each word in list A is used in the story, discuss
    matching it with a word near to it in meaning in list B.

    A   *mistrust* (1.16)   *reclaiming* (1.53)   *wrested* (1.54)
        territory (1.54)   *chores* (1.66)   *petrified* (1.82)   *turmoil* (1.83)
        askew (1.89)   *flutter* (1.97)   *debris* (1.103)
    B   flap   area   upheaval   disbelief   rubbish   taken   panic-
        stricken   recovering   twisted   tasks

3   Which other word in the same row do you think is nearest in
    meaning to the first one in the row?

    contact (1.20)   touch   friend   agreement
    splayed (1.69)   covered   spread   used
    myriad (1.69)   countless   decorated   confusing
    haltingly (1.132)   endlessly   shyly   hesitantly
    tread (1.164)   cord   clothe   step
    bustle (1.184)   hump   explode   hurry
    trespasser (1.195)   agent   intruder   farmer
    heedless (1.211)   unconcerned   stupid   asleep
    ooze (1.219)   sigh   leak   moisten

4   With the given meaning of one word of each pair, discuss what the
    other word might mean.

exceed = go beyond what should be
excessive (1.7) =

permanent = lasting for all time
impermanent (1.63) =

repeat = say or do once more
repetitive (1.100) =

investigate = search to find out
investigator (1.193) =

mature = ripen or develop
maturity (1.9) =

disintegrate = break up into little bits
disintegration (1.83) =

tolerate = put up with or be patient with
tolerant (1.174) =

gorged = filled up or stuffed
disgorged (1.204) =

5   Which words in the story do you think have these meanings?

   a)   stay on and use what is not yours
   b)   put out of a place
   c)   get back what was lost
   d)   a share or amount of the whole
   e)   payment in return for what was taken away
   f)   holding on without letting go
   g)   in a testing or trying out way
   h)   speaking with a lot of unnecessary and useless words
   i)   acts of destruction
   j)   bound to happen

6   Use a good dictionary to find out exactly what these mean.

   humour (1.54)   *rivulets* (1.70)   *fissures* (1.70)   *moorings* (1.81)
   mound (1.103)

Beaming out

Do you like any one of these ideas to work on this week?

1   Go out and look at a man or woman that you see begging or lying destitute on a pavement or anywhere else. Observe his or her appearance and actions closely, and try to imagine a story of his or her past life. Think of some particular happening that finally made him or her homeless and having no kith or kin to get help or support from.

   Begin to write the story of that person by showing him or her in a place at a time when everything was going well. Continue the story by narrating different scenes, up to the one with the person on the pavement or wherever.

2   Imagine a few days of heavy rain; then a landslide bringing down a

large part of a hill and causing some damage and destruction.

Write a story of the rain and the landslide and the people with yourself as the narrator of the events. That is, using the pronoun *I* to tell the story.

3   Make up a story about a person who once owned an estate of coconuts or citrus fruits but lost everything when a hurricane destroyed it all and the bank took away the land for debts that the person owed.

Write the story from the coming of the hurricane to whatever end you wish to give it, but as *scenes* as much as possible and not as *summary*, except where that is necessary.

11 THE COACHMAN AND THE CAB
A. N. Forde

Tuning in

Grown-ups often look back on their childhood and remember pranks
they played. Certain things seemed then to be attractive and adven-
turous.

In this story the coachman took it as a game when some boys used to
shoot seeds at him and jump on the coach and he had to get them off.
But one day something happened.

(A *coach* or *cab* is a vehicle which used to be pulled by
horses—nowadays they have engines. A *catapult* is also called a
sling-shot.)

———

I f you happened to be going towards Bridgetown and you went by
way of Tweedside Road, you would be sure to come to the big iron
gates of Clarke's Funeral Establishment on your right hand. You
couldn't miss it: it occupied a large rectangular area and a wide paved
5 open space in front of the buildings.

In those days we played as children in the narrow roads off
Tweedside, away from the busy rush of the main street. We shot birds
and pitched marbles and interfered with the old and the odd. And we
had a less than humane interest in the horses and coaches of Clarke's
10 Establishment. Every morning the grooms would clean the sleek
skins of the horses and brush the bushy tails and whenever the grooms
turned their backs to us we would slip through the wide gate and,
ducking behind a coach or a cart with grass for the animals, would
sting the horses with 'shac-shac' seeds from our catapults. The
15 grooms would curse us and we would scamper away delighted.

Then there were the funeral coaches and the cab: the cab leaning on
its two forward shafts like an idle labourer on elbow at a bar, the
coaches erect like great black beetles. We didn't like the funeral
coaches.

20 But the cab! That did not belong to the grim world of death and we
liked it; it seemed to promise everlastingly-swift, jolly-bumping,
skimming rides and we envied the tourists who travelled in it over the
island. The top would be swept back and the air would race through it.
The coachman who sat high on it seemed a gay caballero and indeed he
25 was; he drank more than was good for his complexion and he wore a
flushed mottled look at all times; in his cups his face became tomato-
red. Jonno (that was his name) never refused a drink and often you
would see horse-and-cab outside one of the rum-shops, the horse

restlessly dismissing flies while the master 'chopped' liquor inside.
Sometimes the horse would be left champing grass outside the house
of one of Jonno's friends. On such occasions we would climb gently
into the cab and sit anxiously on the high coachman's seat or on the
'cushiony' seat for passengers. We would reach out tentatively to the
long flexible reins that lay wrapped around a projection in front of
Jonno's seat, but courage would fly from us and our eyes vigilantly
watching the doorway through which Jonno had passed would warn
us to skip out on the further side as his red face emerged into the
sunlight. An oath would escape his lips as he spotted us and tumbled in
our direction; but he would soon give up the chase, and our light
laughter would follow the cab disappearing down the lane.

Jonno was our pal as only someone against whom you're accustomed to launch your pranks can be a pal. It used to be fun to shoot
seeds at his black top-hat. We would hide behind a tamarind tree or
hibiscus hedge and let him have it. The solid crack as we found our
mark sent a thrill through us. Jonno would shake his fist at us and
continue on his way—pointless chasing us. Had we wanted to, we
could always have dodged through the barrel of his legs: it was a joke
how wide apart his legs were: a relic of his early jockey days, he said. It
was difficult to see the jockey of the past in his fat round figure, but he
wielded his whip with a flourish that spoke of long experience.

Jonno gained our liking especially because he never told tales to our
parents. He could 'stick his ground'. I can speak truthfully about this
because one day a catapult shot from too nervous a hand hit him in the
face, somewhere deadly near his eye. He had been just about to climb
up to his seat in the cab when our marksman did the trick. The foot he
had on the carriage step had come slowly back down to earth and we
waited. He turned in our direction—this time we were hiding behind
a garbage bin—and in an awful voice he said, slowly:

'The day I put hand on one o' you slimy brutes I goin to break you
neck.'

Rooted to the spot, we feared the present—and the future. There
was no light-footed scampering away, no light-hearted laughter.
Suppose he told our parents. The sky had become dark. We waited,
but nothing farther came of it and we thanked our lucky stars that
Jonno had sought no reprisals. We never shot seeds at his hat again.

Then one day Cecil fell and broke his arm. It happened like this. To
take the place of our lost shooting-practice, we hit on a new idea. We
would slip out of the hiding-place as the cab jogged past and leap on to
it at the back, hanging on for a dear twenty or thirty yards. By the end
of that distance Jonno would be on to us and his whip would
'lightning' through the air and crack explosively like some lissom
firework over our heads and we would jump off the cab precipitately.

I don't think Jonno intended it but this time when he swung the

whip his aim was sure and it struck Cecil a blow across the cheek.
75 Cecil released his hands prematurely and fell, hard. Some yards away
Gerald and I saw the whole thing happen. Gerald, a wriggling
dumpling of eight years' mischief, grabbed my arm anxiously and we
ran on unsteady feet to Cecil who lay in the dusty road. A swelling was
already apparent on his cheek and his face was shot through with pain.
80 He was holding his arm and muttering to himself.

'Can't bend it, man: can't bend it, man.'

His eyes searched our faces and I saw that he was trembling. We
raised him up wondering what would be the next step. This was a new
unrehearsed situation. And Jonno hadn't even stopped! The cab had
85 already swung into the main road and disappeared.

This was awkward and called for something more than the accustomed lie. What tale should (or could) we tell? Suppose his arm was
broken, how could we explain it? A broken arm wasn't something
you could go into a huddle over and fix. It was beyond casual
90 invention.

We half-lifted him and stumbled towards his home, our minds
ticking away but registering nothing on the dial. We reached his home
and his mother asked with the cold knife-point of a voice:

'What happed wid he now!'
95 She was scrubbing over a tub filled with clothes and soapy water.
She didn't interrupt her work but her hands went on rhythmically
squelching the wet garments on the washing-board.

'I ask what happen with he now!'

There was a heavy pause.
100 'He fall down,' I weakly managed.

She wrung out a dripping hunk of clothes, dropped it on the
scrubbing-board, and rose from her bent position over the tub.

'He fall?' Disbelief, not inquiry. She was towering over us now like
some dark queen of the forests. We stood, halting of tongue.
105 'He just stand up and fall, I suppose,' she said.

'He was playing with us. Running,' Gerald ventured but he
couldn't have convinced a rabbit with that uneasy manner.

'How he get that scrape cross his face? Somebody was playing with
him?' I was watching her strong fingers dripping drop by drop with
110 the soap lather, and her wedding-ring shone in the sun. She dropped
her hands from her 'kimbo' and her bangles made jingling music.

Then swiftly, decisively, she grabbed Cecil and gave him a resounding slap on the ear with the wet palm of her hand. Cecil stood
still, cowering, reduced to a cypher, our Cecil, the initiator of every
115 boyish crime, the brain behind our organisation, stood there a mere
clod before her, devoid of identity.

'I fall off the cab,' he said. Tonelessly.

The last Gerald and I saw of them was the piston-like regularity of a

beating arm and the pound of a wet twisted garment on Cecil's
20 unresisting body.

Cecil was taken to the hospital, we heard the next day, and had been detained. It was a complicated fracture, they said.

We entered the hospital some days later, Gerald and I. It was our first visit to Cecil. He was propped up on pillows, his arm in a sling
25 and his black face drawn. He had been having fever as well and I didn't like his look. There was no question of our making the patient feel bright: we hadn't reached the age of duplicity when it would be possible to smile and smart together. I fear our talk would not bear recording—a series of anxious pauses and short monotones trailing
30 into silence. We felt responsible for what had happened. We left the hospital uncomfortable children.

I was all the happier therefore when events shortly took a pleasing turn.

We had been accustomed to drawing down the wrath of our elders
135 in this matter of climbing on to moving vehicles. Occasionally we would sit on the back bumper of a motor-car as it was about to start and enjoy a ride on it until its speed developed after some yards when we would leap off. Public opinion did not favour this and we reluctantly gave it up. But riding behind the cab was surely, we felt,
140 not as harmful and we had switched to that as a concession to adult stodginess.

When Cecil's accident occurred, we expected—and received—a chorus of I-told-you-so voices. My mother confined me to barracks for four days, my first leave being granted when I went to see Cecil at
145 the hospital. Gerald's 'old man' used a more forceful, less psychological technique and a swollen eye accompanied Gerald around for a few days after the encounter. Apparently adults didn't appreciate a spirit of adventure.

I had resumed the normal privileges of citizenship and Gerald's
150 black eye looked more recognisable for what it used to be when Cecil's mother stopped me on one of my morning duty patrols and asked me how I was. I thought this a trifle unusual but answered brightly nevertheless that I was well. I asked how Cecil was.

'He'll be out in two days' time,' she said. And then she went on:
155 'But Jonno isn't even come to say he sorry 'bout what happen to the boy. Wait till my eye clap on he red face,' and gradually from these and other words that we heard later, Gerald and I realised that the burden of general opinion was gradually switching to our side against Jonno. They were calling Jonno a worthless scamp 'to knock the boys off the
160 cab and go on 'bout he business, widout even coming and asking if anybody get hurt.' 'After all, boys will be boys,' they said. 'You can't treat them like animals.'

We smiled inwardly at this sign that the wind was blowing in our

favour: we were almost heroes now. It was a welcome change from
165 less palmy days.

Meanwhile I felt a twinge of disappointment myself over Jonno's
behaviour. Not a sign, not a word had come from him. In fact we
hadn't seen him since Cecil's accident. Nor was the cab ever at
Clarke's Establishment when we looked in. It had vanished off the
170 skin of the earth. Nobody seemed to know where Jonno was either.
The old drunkard, they said.

And then one evening two days later, I saw a pair of bow legs slowly
coming up the road and my eyes strained to make probability sure.
Instinctively I looked for the cab . . . but there was none. I couldn't
175 mistake the bow-legged figure in the black top-hat: It was Jonno. He
was limping.

He came up to me, paused, and looked at me closely. Absently I
noticed a piece of adhesive tape stuck along his cheek.

'It wasn't you fall off the cab,' he said. 'No, it couldn't be; they say
180 his arm broken,' he answered himself. This slant sounded a bit queer
to me.

'Yes, his arm broken. You didn't know?' I asked.

'Did my whip hit him?' He asked ignoring my question.

'Yes,' I said.

185 'Is he home?' Apparently he was going to pretend ignorance of the
whole affair.

'He came home yesterday,' I said. 'But how you don't know all o'
this?'

'He was in hospital?'

190 'Where else?' I asked.

He seemed to be pondering this one out.

Then: 'But I was there nearly two weeks myself. Came out this
morning.'

I couldn't believe it. True there wasn't any smell of rum hanging
195 around him. So something must have taken place.

'Had an accident Tuesday before last . ∴. with a car,' he continued.

Tuesday before last, I thought. That was the day Cecil had had the
fall.

'Was in hospital ever since . . . my hip,' and he ran his hand down
200 and along his buttocks, as if to verify what he had said.

'Cecil and you were in hospital at the same time?' I asked; 'It appears
so,' he said. 'I didn't know till this morning.' It sounded fantastic, but
he could hardly be lying. For one thing the adhesive tape along his
cheek suggested an accident of some sort. And his limp.

205 'And the cab?' I asked, still hoping to trap him into some self-
evident falsehood.

'Broken up. Shafts and wheels useless.'

'No,' I said. almost instinctively, hoping it wasn't true.

'Yes,' he said quietly.

'Where this happened?' I asked.

'In My Lord's Hill. They brought the cab down yesterday. It's in the Establishment.' There was no doubt about his telling the truth. I ceased further questioning.

He left me soon after this on his way to Cecil's mother. I heard afterwards from Cecil (whose arm, by the way, mended very well) that Jonno had to use every rhetorical gift to defend himself from Ma Cecil's bitter onslaught. Even bodily harm was threatened him, but truth prevailed, and he was eventually allowed—reluctantly, I gather—to leave her presence intact.

As for the cab I saw it that very evening in a corner of the open quadrangle in front of the Establishment. Amidst the bustle of Tweedside Road, it stood unsheltered from sun and weather, leaning backwards on its haunches, its two wheels figureless, its split shafts like broken arms in prayer.

Without its coachman it seemed hopelessly empty of appeal, lost; and he, without it, was an alien on foot, no whirling whip, no high perch to lend him glamour. Together they had seemed to link the old and the gay with newer and swifter age. Separated they had become merely part of the rubble of the past.

Talking about it

A   *The events of the story*

1   Why did the cab attract the boys?
2   What did they try to do on it whenever Jonno left it outside a house?
3   What tells you that Jonno never meant to do the boys any harm?
4   Why did the boys like Jonno?
5   Why did they stop shooting seeds at his hat?
6   In those days cars had bumpers you could sit on. Why did they stop getting on the bumpers of motor cars? What did they start doing then?
7   What made Cecil fall from the cab and break his arm?
8   What were the boys worried about more than Cecil's pain when he broke his arm?
9   How did Cecil's mother take it when he came home with the broken arm?
10 What seemed strange to the boys when Cecil had to take his mother's beating?
11 What punishment did the narrator's mother give him?
12 After the boys had been punished in different ways, what did people begin to say about Jonno?

13　What did the narrator then begin to think about Jonno?
14　Why had Jonno not shown himself, nor been heard of, all the time Cecil was in hospital?
15　What happened to the cab?
16　At whose home did Jonno have to do a lot of explaining?
17　When the narrator saw the broken-up cab what change took place in how he regarded the coachman and the cab?

B　The writing skills

1　Do you think the story was made up or do you think it actually happened to the author? If you think it was made up, make a guess as to what made the author imagine it.
2　If a hero is someone to be admired or pitied, who is the hero of this story?
3　From whose point of view, or from inside of whom, is the story told:

a)　Cecil's
b)　Jonno's
c)　the narrator's
d)　nobody's

4　Which of these did the writer set out to do when he wrote the story? Do you think he succeeded?

a)　to terrify the reader
b)　to sadden the reader
c)　to amuse the reader
d)　to anger the reader

Do you think there are any details put in by the writer which are not necessary to make the story seem to be happening in a real place with real people?

5　What gives amusement when each of these phrases is used?

a)　*halting of tongue* (1.104)
b)　*a mere clod before her, devoid of identity* (1.115)
c)　*the age of duplicity when it would be possible to smile and smart together* (1.127) (to *smart* is to suffer a little sharp pain).
d)　*resumed the normal privileges of citizenship* (1.149)

C　The use of words

In writing your own stories all the words in this story would be useful to know. But since you cannot master them all at once, pay most attention to those that would be most useful to you now for describing actions and people and things.

1   Try to use these in oral sentences of your own:

scamper (1.15)   *rhythmically* (1.96)   *squelching* (1.97)
ventured (1.106)   *bustle* (1.221)   *rubble* (1.229)

2   Fit these into their missing places in the sentences below:

wielded (1.50)   *casual* (1.89)   *towering* (1.103)   *cowering* (1.114)
instinctively (1.174)   *eventually* (1.218)

   a)   When I saw the stone coming I _____ closed my eyes.
   b)   You do things in a _____ way, never taking care.
   c)   After waiting a long time we _____ got a bus.
   d)   The angry woman _____ a stick at the boys teasing her.
   e)   There was a high building _____ above our heads.
   f)   The little boy was _____ in fright when the storm was
         raging.

3   Which two words in the same row are nearly alike in meaning?

   a)   *sleek* (1.10)   humane   smooth   rhetorical
   b)   *grim* (1.20)   stern   adhesive   lissom
   c)   *mottled* (1.26)   devoid   prevailed   spotted
   d)   *wrath* (1.134)   alien   anger   glamour
   e)   *perch* (1.227)   rest   onslaught   flourish

4   Match a word in list A with a word in list B that has a similar meaning.

   A   *flushed* (1.26)   *muttering* (1.80)   *interrupt* (1.96)   *bustle* (1.221)
   B   grumbling   jostle   reddish   break

5   Which other word in each row is most *opposite* in meaning to the first one in the row?

   a)   *delighted* (1.15)   complicated   confined   displeased
   b)   *flexible* (1.34)   unbendable   detained   unrehearsed
   c)   *emerged* (1.37)   entered   apparent   resounding
   d)   *reluctantly* (1.218)   vigilantly   prematurely   eagerly
   e)   *vanished* (1.169)   resumed   appeared   sought

Beaming out

Here are three ideas which could be used for writing stories. Choose one of them or some other idea of your own and try to write a story this week to keep in your folder and to discuss with your teacher and friends.

1   Jonno was part of the scenes when the boys shot seeds at him, when he left the cab outside a house, when a boy fell off the cab, and so on. He was not part of the scene with the boys at Cecil's home, nor of what happened at the narrator's house, and so on.

Write a story about the boys and Jonno, with Jonno as the narrator describing those scenes he was involved in, and give your story a title you think suits it best.

2   Think of a personal adventure you were involved in once, when you had fun but got into a little bit of trouble—or imagine something like that happening to someone—and you had to face your mother or father or somebody like that.

Write the story of the scene when the thing happened and the scene with the person or persons afterwards. Try to tell it as amusingly as you can.

3   Think about this as the title of a story, *Three in a Jam,* and make up some events that you think a story with that title could have in it.

Then write the story of the scenes you imagine.

12 NO MOURNING IN THE VALLEY
Vic Reid

Tuning in

Do you think you can remain cool in the face of great danger? Will you be able to think quickly and have steady nerves to use skill to save yourself? Will you save someone else first, even though you might not be able to save yourself?

In this story a boy's devotion and skill and intelligence come into play, but the people of the valley get ready to mourn for him.

———

After the New Year the sough of the north wind died out of the tall cedars on the Blue Mountains and evening was cold and misty no longer. Then filling all the hollows of the mountains and flowing gently up and down the slopes came the white glow of the Easter lilies,
5 bringing such a peace and hope that almost the river was of no consequence.

But the old men whittling at their doorways in the Valley and cocking an eye at the thunderhead hanging over the peaks and an ear to the voice of the river, nodded their heads and said to all who would
10 ask: 'Man-O, watch the river.'

Yet, the river was beautiful. The beauty of a wilding horse, unbridled and foaming at the lips, the river when it tumbled into the Valley. And yet, so broad and softly, with graceful loopings and easy flow did the river approach the Valley as it rolled along the tableland
15 above, lapping at the roots of yacca and mahogany, rolling over and chuckling with the smoothly round stones which had found a bed in its path, loving the fat mountain grasses that plucked at the edge of its shining coat in a manner teasingly coy. But all this was before it breasted the edge of the tableland and plunged into the Valley below.
20

Many people lived in the Valley. There were the families of Logan, and of Goodison, and Charley Greaves' widowed children, and of Pastor Timothy McGovern who wore a white turban on the Sabbath, and yes, there was Rupe.
25 Rupe had no family. He had tumbled into the Valley almost as abruptly as the river. It was this way.

One day the family of Logan was ploughing the half acre behind the house. In the Logan family, there was Mass Bob Logan and his wife and their daughter, Noreen. Noreen was of a beauty unmatched in the
30 Valley. Evening, and the twinkle of stars just beyond the dusk, these

were Noreen when she smiled and the dark velvet of her face was illumined with the whole goodness of her . . .

How easy it is to be taken on apace when talking about the river or
35 Noreen! Almost you would forget that this tale is about Rupe—almost, except that once you have known Rupe there can be no forgetting him.

So now, the family of Logan were ploughing into the half acre behind
40 the house where there were cabbages and lettuce and garden eggs and okroes, convenient to the kitchen. It was during this ploughing that they met Rupe. Noreen it was who heard him first.

'What was that?' she asked as she rested the tines of the fork in the furrow and looked around her. The shrill cry came again. She pushed
45 the fork away. 'It is a baby!' she cried.

Her father tilted his ragged coconut-straw hat forward over his eyes and rubbed the back of his head.

'A baby?' he asked, peering up at her from under the brim of his hat. 'A baby? Heh, heh.' He looked at Mrs Logan.
50 'Then what would a baby be doing up here now?' asked Mrs Logan.

Mr Logan laughed again. 'A baby in our half acre? Heh, heh. Then mean to say if we had a baby we wouldn't know, Mrs Logan?'

But Noreen did not stop to hear her father's little joke. She was breasting through the tender shoots of congo peas, hastily pushing her
55 feet through the mulch of damp grasses that covered the roots—and was out and stooping to the tiny bundle on the bank of the stream which branched from the mighty river. There she saw Rupe. He was then somewhat under a year old.

That was over twelve years ago and now Rupe was a grown boy.
60 His origin? Nobody was sure. But the good and sensible guess was that he was the unwanted child of some city woman who had come to the Valley the day before with a picknicking crowd, and had wrapped the baby in warm clothing and had left him near the house of the Logans in the certainty that he would be found. But whatever was his
65 origin, Rupe grew well and strong and loved Noreen with a love that never questioned, never tried to understand, always satisfied just to be near her.

And was Rupe clever? Lord, you ought to see him. You ought to see him at cricket on the village green, or shooting birds with his catapult,
70 or pitching marbles in a dizzy ring-and-toss, or swinging from the vines of the great banyan tree which grew near the river, or swimming in the river.

And that was where he excelled—pitting his strength against the river. He swam like a fish; threshing through the surging flow with a
75 scything overarm and a powerful kick that put him across the

strongest currents in a manner that was amazing to see. They even made up a little name for him. Rupe the Waterman, they called him.

The old year had turned with a bluster of winds and a flurry of rain that blew right into the new year. In February the rain ceased, and only the redness of the sky at dawn and sunset made the old men of the village purse their lips and shake their heads and say, 'No good will come of this weather.'

'Man-O,' they said in the village square at evening when the sun rolled away with its cohorts of heavy clouds streaked in black and red; 'Man-O,' they said, 'Jehovah has covered His face with vexness. Trouble will come to the land before Easter, mark my word.'

But soon it was Lent, and thoughts turned to the ginger cropping and to the creamy yellow yams maturing under the rich earth. Ginger knives were sharpened and soon they would be flashing about the noduled roots.

The first days of spring went by and clouds had gone from the shoulder of the mountain, and now the days were hot and clear. Easter lilies were filling the hollows and flowing gently up the slopes, and for a time fear left those who had known bad times when the river grew angry in the Valley.

'Rupe, you will go fishing today?'

That was from Noreen, smiling Noreen going on to be twenty and filled to overflowing with the indefinable essence of rich young womanhood. There was a catch at the throat when Noreen went by, for in her lithe grace and heart-shaped face, her ready gentleness and swift little kindnesses, the humble villagers saw the fulfilment of the promise in the Good Book about angels entertained unawares. To them, she was an angel.

'Rupe, boy, you going fishing today, eh?'

Rupe looked up into the blue clearness of the sky. He nodded.

'A good day for fishing,' he agreed. He looked at her. 'And better still if Sister Noreen will come with me.'

Noreen smiled and shook her head. Rupe smiled and spoke again.

'We might catch a fat mullet and turn him over the hot stoves to roast. I know a place where the cocoes are fit, soft and melting in the mouth. How now, Sister Noreen? Roasted cocoes and mullet for lunch—you will come, yes?'

That was Rupe, wheedling her. There was never a day's fishing so much fun as the days when Noreen went with him to the river.

Noreen laughed. 'Boy, there's too much to do today. Think I can waste a day at the river with you?'

'How now, Sister Noreen—even for a little while, yes? The river is singing today!'

Ah, the river was singing today, he said. Noreen remembered the bright days when the river sang with a multiple of tongues among the stones in the shallows. Music, it was. Sometimes you fell asleep with its soft notes wandering around in your ears and never was sleep more restful, more restoreful; nor ever a waking more like heaven than to wake with this music at your ear.

'Boy, how can I go with so much work to do?'

She couldn't give in. Spring was here and there was much to do.

'Very well, Sister Noreen. Tell you what we will do. You come and stay awhile with me and I will return with you and help with the ginger.'

Well, there it was. That was an easy way to solve the problem. She laughed heartily. 'Boy, but a clever one you are! Alright, alright, I will come to the river with you.'

So they went to the river, he with his bamboo pole and basket and whistling a gay tune, and she holding her scarf that whipped in the wind about her neck, and laughing with the sun on her face. They passed the banyan tree and Rupe leaped and caught the vine in one bound that swung him to the great crotch of the tree: then, laughing, he swung back to the ground again by the river's edge.

'Rupe, you mind you break your neck!' Noreen cried in alarm. But Rupe only laughed some more, for he knew the vine was strong.

At the river's edge Rupe struck for mullet, expertly flicking the line so it floated naturally downstream and enticed the fat mountain mullets to wriggle after the bait. Truly, it was a good day for fishing.

Beside him on the grassy bank, the silver scales took up more and more room. Noreen hummed snatches of songs as her knife whisked over them, removing the scales and readying them for the pot when they returned home. After a while she climbed to the top of a rock and dozed with the music of the river in her ear.

Fish was running beautifully, and Rupe was too engrossed in the play of his line to notice that after all these weeks the big, black clouds were boiling up from behind the mountain, spewing out of the passes, were climbing back to their stand on the shoulder of the mountain. Nor did he notice when the dreadful black roof opened above the mountain, and sheets and torrents of water poured on the head of the river, swelling the flow to a turgidity that lashed and tore at the mountain-bed, bounding and sweeping down the race, smashing and rending at mighty rocks and old trees, bruting the fat mountain grasses that had lovingly plucked at its shining coat—and tumbled into the Valley below.

There was fear in the Valley. There were men, old men, who had once seen the river at flood and knew the terror of those moments when the main stream divided into a hundred streams, each as terrible, each cutting its own channel between the rocks and the highlands, mowing down the houses and trees in its path, slashing through the Valley like so many scythes wielded by giant hands; not ceasing until they had joined bank to bank and covered the whole Valley in a winding-sheet of water beneath which many people of the Valley had lain quiet and still.

Rupe was resting on the bank with his hat over his face and the rod held between his fingers and toes. The day had turned quite still and the somnolent humming of the river insects made him drowsy. It was not until it had been going on for some time that he felt the heavy drag on his line. He sat up.

Far up the river he heard the low roar. He didn't know what to make of it. In his own short lifetime he had never heard the roar of heavy water, and now he thought that what he heard were muted noises from the thunderheads which hung over the mountain.

But the river was flowing faster and faster and fishing was now impossible. He commenced to reel in his line. With a little wonder at the rapid rising of the river, he saw the water lapping up the bank past his feet. Suddenly, he looked around him. Where was Noreen?

'Sister Noreen?' he called, winding at his bamboo spool. 'Sister Noreen?'

Noreen was lying in the sun atop the rock. The voice of the river soothed her in sleep.

She must have gone home while I dozed, thought Rupe, remembering that she had the ginger to peel. The water was swiftly rising, swirling about his knees. *Noreen must have gone home*, he thought.

He gathered in the line and looked around for the basket of fish. It had been swept away. He sent a glance downstream and there he saw the basket of beautiful mullet caught in a hollow at the foot of a large rock. He saw that the water had risen dangerously high, but he was determined not to lose his fish. There was only one thing to do, to go after it as quickly as possible. Half wading, half swimming, he reached the rock. He fumbled at the basket which had entangled its weave among the brambles. He pulled and tugged while the water beat his body against the rock. By the time the basket was free, he was panting for breath. He knew he could not swim the river with the rod and basket, and he a tired boy, so he thought he would climb to the top of the rock where he would rest awhile. So, he clambered to the top, and there he saw Noreen.

'Noreen!' he cried in amazement. 'Sister Noreen?'

She awakened at his voice, blinked a little and then sat up smiling while she patted her hair into place. Then full wakefulness came to her and she heard the river.

The water was now all about them. It lashed and curled like a million whips, foamed and hissed in massive rage, gathering itself in darkling anger through which the stripped trunks of murdered trees gleamed whitely before they were sucked down into the vortex. There was no stopping the rising river. Like a creeping death, it inched and inched up the rock, spraying them with cold kisses.

Noreen remembered the stories she had heard of the river. She covered her face with her palms in horror at the sight of the cruel monstrous thing which the lovely river had become. Rupe saw her there, rocking her shoulders to the grievous rhythm of her terrified heart. He too remembered the stories of the flood. In his mind he saw the flood sweeping over the rock, and she a girl and not able to swim. If Noreen went, there would be mourning in the Valley. There would be such tears from the Logans and the Goodisons and Charley Greaves' widowed children and all the people of the Valley; and Pastor McGovern's voice would take on the quiver which it did whenever he read the awful words of the burial service. The sun would be dark and there would be many voices raised in mourning.

'Sister Noreen, don't cry,' he called above the noise of the river.

Rupe looked across the raging water. There was no place for refuge. The river had divided into many tongues, each seeking its own prey. Then he noticed the banyan, standing in full strength and scorning the water dashing around its feet while its vines trailed gracefully in the stream.

Quickly he shook out his rod, eyeing the distance to the tree. Standing with his legs well apart, he sought out a vine which was not too stout for his thin line to tow across the current. It was a good forty feet away. He looped the line about his left hand, settled the bamboo rod in his hand so it nudged against the heel of his palm. He whirled the rod above his head . . . *one* . . . *two* . . . *three*—he made the cast.

The line was away, bellying out across the water. He held his breath as the line whipped upstream. It hit the water and commenced drifting downstream towards the tree. Rupe crouched on top of the rock, watching the play of the line as it acknowledged every ripple, and for a shocking instant he thought the hook might fail to snag the vine at which he was aiming. But with a quick jerk, it caught.

Slowly, carefully, he drew in the line, bringing in the vine until he could lean over and hold it fast. Then he called to Noreen.

'Sister Noreen take hold here and you can swing to the tree. You can be safe there.'

But when Noreen looked up at his words and saw the great tree which seemed so far away and the raging water underneath, she shook her head violently.

'No—no—!' she gasped. 'I—I'll be drowned!'

She buried her face in her hands again. Rupe did not hesitate, not

clever Rupe. He would not give her more time to argue, and she a girl
and liking to argue. Swiftly he looped the vine about her waist and
made it fast with the line, binding knots he had learnt in the scout
troop. Then, never hesitating, he pushed her mightily from the rock.
260 Noreen arched through the air, a scream bursting from her lips. Her
feet brushed the water, then she was going up, up, and had swung into
the leafy refuge. She clutched at the branches and hauled herself into
the great crotch. Rupe sighed in relief. Sister Noreen was safe. There
would be no mourning in the Valley. Then he stooped for the rod to
265 fish a vine for himself.

But the rod was not on the rock. He had momentarily forgotten the
water breaking over the rock and the rod had been swept away.

Now safe in the banyan tree, Noreen quickly saw the danger Rupe
was in.

270 'Rupe: Rupe! she screamed above the roar of the river. 'Rupe!
Hurry! Hurry—the water's rising!'

There could be no hurrying for Rupe. He was marooned on the
rock with the water rising fast and no way of saving himself. Noreen
alternately wept and screamed his name. She watched the water climb
275 to his knees, watching him struggle to keep his footing while the
water climbed higher, and higher. Then in the space of the blink of an
eye-lid, Rupe had disappeared from the rock.

Later, when the water had subsided, the villagers rescued her from the
280 banyan tree. Between her moanings and her tears, they heard of the
hero Rupe had been before he had been swept away. Slowly they
returned to the village, their feet sloshing through the oozy mud.
Slowly, in mourning they returned, mourning the loss of their little
friend and crying that such a tombstone they would build for him that
285 the world would see all his brave young life eternally written in stone.
All this they talked of, while their feet sucked through the mud and the
lonely cries of the kling-kling pierced the great quietness of the Valley.

But do you think Rupe was drowned? Whatever are you saying?
Don't make me laugh. Have you forgotten the clever little boy whom
290 they named Rupe the Waterman who could swim like a fish? Eh,
really you must have forgotten.

Why—by the time they reached the first houses on the edge of the
village with their throats thickened in sorrow, whom did they see,
wet, bedraggled and battered, but Rupe. Battered but fully alive, there
295 was the boy they had mourned. Why—he had swum that river all the
way downstream until he came to a highland and there rested until the
water went down. And here he was running towards Noreen.

'Sister Noreen! Sister Noreen!'

Then such a laughing and a dancing was there that you would have
300 thought it was an August Fair!

96

'Rupe! Rupe, boy! Alive and well you are, boy?'

That was Noreen, crying and laughing at the same time and hugging him to her.

'Praise! Praise Jehovah! Our Rupe is alive!'

But all through the dancing and the crying and laughter, there was Rupe shaking his head and bemoaning that he had lost his rod. Such a rod it had been, there never could be another like it, Rupe said. Forty feet, a full forty feet he had made his cast for the vine. Could there be another like it?

But the villagers laughed.

'How now, Rupe? A rod is it you want, boy? Then we will give you a rod! Such a rod as you had never seen!' cried the villagers.

And so it was. With the money with which they would have cut his name in stone, they sent to the town and bought him a fine rod from the big store, long and limber and balanced so he could make a cast fully *sixty* feet up the stream. And that summer, he caught many fishes with it, did Rupe.

Talking about it

A   *The events of the story*

1   Who was Rupe, and who was Noreen?
2   Why were the old men worried about the river?
3   What skills was Rupe very good at?
4   How did he get Noreen to go fishing with him that day?
5   When Rupe got drowsy what caused a heavy drag on his line to make him sit up?
6   What was making the low roar far up the river?
7   Why did Rupe not know what the roar meant?
8   Why did Noreen not tell him what was happening?
9   How did Rupe come to discover that Noreen was still there asleep on the rock?
10   *There was no place for refuge* (1.230). What does that mean?
11   Why did Rupe send his line upstream? What was he trying to do?
12   How did Noreen get across the raging water of the river to the safety of the bank?
13   How did Rupe get to safety himself?
14   Which particular skill or skills did he use to save Noreen and himself?

B   *The writing skills*

1   Is the narrator one of the persons in the story or a sort of all-seeing eye?

97

2　Generally speaking a writer must prepare the reader for the ending of a story so that the ending does not seem unlikely and hard to believe. When Rupe uses his fishing and swimming skills to save Noreen and himself we do not find it surprising or hard to believe that he could do it. Why? How did the writer prepare us for that?

3　The writer put in a coincidence or chance happening to explain how Rupe discovered Noreen marooned on the rock just in time. Did you find that easy to believe or not? Why?

4　Does the story have a *conflict* or problem? If so, between whom and whom, or whom and what, or what and what?

5　If the story has a problem or *conflict*, does it have a *climax* where the problem is decided finally one way or another and you know how it is removed?

6　The writer uses *figurative language* quite a lot in this story. He uses words to make comparisons, although he does not state that he is doing so. In other words he uses words *metaphorically*. For example, he said the river was *chuckling with the stones* (1.16), the grasses *plucked at it* (1.17), it had a shining *coat*, and so on.

　　Find some more places where the writer used words metaphorically and discuss whether the *metaphor* or comparison helps you to see or hear or feel better what the writer is describing.

C　*The use of words*

Some of the words used in this story are used very much by people in telling about things that happened. They are used to describe actions, people, places, and things. You must pay attention to them and try to be able to use them. Begin by noticing what meaning each one seems to have in the story.

1　These ten are fairly easy for you to use in oral sentences of your own:

swift (1.103)　*wriggle* (1.145)　*torrents* (1.156)　*swirling* (1.191)
blinked (1.207)　*gleamed* (1.213)　*instant* (1.245)　*violently* (1.253)
sloshing (1.282)　*battered* (1.294)

2　Fit these into the sentences below:

chuckling (1.16)　*engrossed* (1.151)　*spewing* (1.153)
massive (1.212)　*momentarily* (1.266)　*alternately* (1.274)
subsided (1.279)　*bemoaning* (1.306)

  a)　The audience was ＿＿＿＿ at the jokes the comedian made.
  b)　At the funeral they were all ＿＿＿＿ the tragic accident.
  c)　I eased up on the leash ＿＿＿＿ and the dog bounded away.

d)   You were so _____ in what you were doing that you did not hear me call.

e)   A _____ ten-ton truck was bearing down upon us.

f)   We will take turns _____ in keeping guard.

g)   When the flood _____ they were able to get across to the people who had been marooned.

h)   The old car was _____ out of a lot of smoke from its exhaust.

3   What are the missing letters in these words?

whit★ling   il★umined   excel★ed   pit★ing   t★reshing
s★rging   lith★   so★nolent   rip★le   bedrag★led

Beaming out

If you wish you may use one of these ideas for writing a story for your folder this week.

1   Make up a story about a flood that took place somewhere that you are familiar with, in which these words might be used:

thunderhead   surging   streaked   cohorts   swift   torrents
terror   swishing   entangled   brambles   massive   raging
refuge   violently   marooned   subsided   sloshing
bedraggled   battered   bemoaning

Tell about the weather and the characters before the flood occurred, the beginning of the rain, the flooding and an incident in it, and afterwards.

2   Imagine being one of the villagers in Vic Reid's story and you are writing a letter to a friend just after Rupe saved Noreen. Tell the story in your letter as far as you know it and from your own point of view.

3   Make up a person with certain skills and characteristics, and then imagine an incident in which those skills have to be used to avoid danger.

Write the scenes of a story about the persons and his or her actions in the crisis.

13 PIG MONEY
Elizabeth Walcott

Tuning in

How often have you felt you were being treated unfairly? What do you do about it? Do you think girls and women are treated more unfairly than boys and men? Perhaps Ianthe in this story thought so. She shrieked in rebellion as anyone might. What happened afterwards?

———

One of the first things Ianthe could remember was being given a galvanised pail to hold in one hand, and a few coppers wrapped in newspaper to be gripped tightly in the other, and told to go for the hog-food. Every morning early she did this, and again in the late
5 afternoon. Sometimes she staggered back home with what was to her a heavy burden, sometimes she could swing the bucket on the return journey almost as easily as when she set out. It depended on how many of the homes were tenanted in the seaside village near which she lived.
Ianthe's home was a hut set high on a hill overlooking the white-
10 washed, red-roofed houses dotted about on the green-and-brown pasture-land sloping down to the wide beach. Behind her home, the hill rose higher with casuarina groves here and there, and other shabby little houses scattered on its swelling bosom. In front was a vast expanse of ocean, shading from indigo-blue to emerald-green, and a
15 serried line of breakers bursting over the reef on to the beige-coloured sand. The roar of the sea was in Ianthe's ears all day long, forming—had she known it—part of Nature's rhapsody of hill, sea and sky. All around her was displayed a landscape—one of Nature's masterpieces—in glorious extravagant shades of green, blue and
20 white.
But Ianthe cared nought for these things; her mind was too full of pressing daily needs. She must help her mother get water from the stand-pipe, and when the wind, scented with a species of wild verbena that grew profusely over the hillside, became boisterous, she thought,
25 not of its salty fragrance, but of how to hold her own against it as she made her careful, toiling way up the hill with the bucket of water on her head, one small, thin hand unflung to steady it. She must go to the shop further up the hill, but as she went she saw nothing of the charming play of light and shade across the grass, she heard unmoved
30 the mysterious whispering of the casuarinas; she was climbing, not for pleasure, but as part of the day's toil. And, chief task of all, she must go for the hog-food. Even when she grew big enough to go to school,

this still remained part of her day's work. Off she would go, a small brown figure, swinging her bucket and singing cheerfully, if discor-
35 dantly, all the way to the bay-houses; then back she trudged, the sour reek of the bucket's contents proclaiming her task successfully accomplished.

'Poor little thing,' some passer-by might say, but Ianthe would have been surprised, for she herself realised no need of pity. Must not
40 'the hog' be fed? Would not the 'pig money' buy things for her mother and father, her brother Joe, and herself? And had not her mother only the other day explained that she must 'care the hog good' for that was hers—Ianthe's—and the two sheep were Joe's? With great delight Ianthe planned what she would buy with the pig money: chief among
45 those things were a skipping-rope with red handles and a pencil-box with a pen, rubber and a nice long pencil, and a box of coloured chalks. Personal adornment did not as yet appeal to Ianthe, and she was happiest in the smelly old dress she wore when she fetched the hog's-food. She never noticed that the animal was always referred to
50 as 'the hog,' when it came to tending or feeding him, but the profit expected from his sale was spoken of as 'pig money.'

One day as Ianthe came in from an errand to the shop, and set down her basket in the little back shed which served as the kitchens, she heard excited discussion in the front room between her parents and
55 Joe.

'But, Joe, how we goin' manage 'bout yuh clothes?' his mother was asking anxiously.

'Woman, de boy get de scholaship to Highfields and yuh talkin' like if he ain't to tek it up,' his father replied impatiently.
60 'I ain' said nothin' o' de sort,' retorted his wife angrily. 'All I axin' is how we goin' buy clothes fuh he. He cahn' go school widout proper clothes fuh de boys to laugh at he, nuh?'

There was a moment's silence, then: 'Well,' said the father, 'we mus' sell one o' de sheep an' de hog.'
65 'But I tell Ianthe de hog is her own,' objected the mother.

'Cahn help dat,' argued the father. 'It got to sell to buy de t'ings Joe need . . . .'

He got no further. A whirlwind of fury swept into the room.

'He my hog, my hog,' shouted Ianthe. 'I goin' buy a skippin' rope
70 an' a pencil box wid de pig money, an' put down de res' to get clothes fuh me to go to de big school too.'

'Girrl, shut yuh mout',' ordered her father. 'Yuh bruddah win a scholarship an' we got to fix him decent to go nex' term.'

'Ianthe, I goin' buy another hog soon's I kin, chile,' comforted her
75 mother; 'you ain' ready to go to big school yet.'

Ianthe burst into tears. Between her sobs she shrieked; 'Tain' fair, 'tain' fair! I got to walk all de way up an' down de hill fuh de hog-food an' now I ain' gettin' none o' de pig money.'

'Girrl, stop dat noise, an' onderstan' dat yuh bruddah got brains, an'
dey might bring him in de chance to go high. One day he might get in
de House!'

All this time Joe said nothing. He regarded the scene with a mixture
of pity and dismay, lest after all the precious pig money might not be
forthcoming; pity for Ianthe who had to be sacrificed for him.
Timidly he approached his sister. 'Ianthe . . .,' he began; but she cried
louder and pulled away from him.

Wearily the mother got up and left the room. She went into the
back-shed and returned with the bucket. The resignation of ages was
on her face and in her voice as she went over to Ianthe and said, 'Tain'
no use, chile; they ain' no otha way to get de money. And it time to go
fuh de hog-food.' She tried to push the bucket handle into the child's
hand.

'Ain' goin' fuh no hog-food agin,' stormed Ianthe, kicking the
bucket out of her mother's hand. It clattered out on to the front step.

Her father went into action. 'Now, none o' dat,' he threatened, with
uplifted hand. 'You jes' pick up dat bucket an' go fuh dat hog-food.'

Ianthe looked at him through her tears. If she refused, that heavy
hand would descend upon her with a stinging blow. She glanced at her
mother; her face was sad but stern. She looked at her brother, tears
were streaming down his face. Ianthe had never heard the saying 'Men
must work and women must weep' but at that moment she accepted
its purport with her inmost being.

Still crying loudly, she picked up the bucket and set out. Her hat had
fallen off, and Joe now ran after her with it.

'Ianthe, here's your hat,' he called, and placed it on her head. For a
moment the two children looked into each other's tearful eyes.

'Ianthe,' stammered the boy, 'when I'm a man, I promise, I promise
. . .' Words failed him.

'What yuh promise?' asked his sister curiously.

But the boy could find no words to express his intention—all he
wanted to do for himself, for his parents, and above all, for Ianthe who
had to give up her pig money to help him to go to the big school.

All he could say was: 'Yuh shan't have to go fuh no mo' hog-food.'

Ianthe wiped her eyes with a corner of her dirty dress. 'Yuh goin' to
do good at school, Joe? Yuh goin' be a great man like Pappie say?'

'Hope so,' answered Joe.

'Well, I better go,' said the girl picking up the bucket. 'Somebody
got to go fuh de dog-food.'

Joe watched her until she reached the first house and disappeared
behind it. Then he turned towards home, and as he went he kept on
saying to himself: 'Po' lil Ianthe, some day I'll mek up fuh dis.'

But Ianthe, her moment of rebellion past, was at that moment knocking at the kitchen–door and calling meekly to the cook: 'I come fuh de hog-food.'

Talking about it

A *The events of the story*

1 Where did Ianthe live?
2 What was her job every morning?
3 What pleasant things around her did she not notice?
4 To whom did the pig belong?
5 What did Ianthe want to do with the money when the pig was sold?
6 What did her father decide to do with the money?
7 What reason did he have for that?
8 How did Ianthe's brother, Joe, feel about his father's decision?
9 What did Ianthe do to show how she felt?
10 What did her father do then?
11 How did Joe show how sorry he was?
12 How did Ianthe show that she was satisfied that Joe should get the money?

B *The writing skills*

1 In which part of the story is the *style* easier to read, and in which part it is a little difficult for you?
2 Is the *conflict* in the story between

    a)   Ianthe and her father?
    b)   Ianthe and her brother?
    c)   different feelings inside of Ianthe?

3 Which *character* in a well-known fairy tale does Ianthe remind you of?
4 Why does the writer have the characters in this story speak in that way, and not in correct English?
5 Which part of the story is written as *summary* and which part is written as *scene*?
6 What do you suppose the writer wants you to think about as the *theme* of the story?
7 Did the writer prepare you for Ianthe's change of heart at the end? Was there anything shown before about Ianthe that could explain it?
8 Why do you suppose the writer made a point of telling that Ianthe never saw the beauty around her?
9 Where do you suppose is the *climax* of the story?
10 Would you agree that this story is like a parable?

C *The use of words*

1 From the way the words in list A are used in the story you can easily get a good idea of what each means. Look for a word in list B to pair with one in list A that is nearest to it in meaning.

A *burden* (l.6)   *expanse* (l.14)   *displayed* (l.18)   *trudged* (l.35)
   reek (l.36)   *retorted* (l.60)   *shrieked* (l.76)   *clattered* (l.94)
B replied   area   screamed   load   smell   showed
   plodded   rattled

2 Think about how the first word of each row is used in the story and look for another word in the same row that is like it in meaning.

tenanted (l.8)   painted   occupied   visited
breakers (l.15)   shirts   stones   waves
extravagant (l.19)   wide   rich   dull
profusely (l.24)   plentifully   simply   slowly
boisterous (l.24)   large   noisy   heavy
fragrance (l.25)   prettiness   uselessness   scent
accomplished (l.36)   done   taken   stolen
adornment (l.47)   decoration   wisdom   ambition
dismay (l.83)   chase   alarm   anger
timidly (l.85)   loudly   nervously   perfectly

Beaming out

Are you interested in doing one of these?

1 From your own experience make up a person who was entitled to something but was denied it when the time came for him or her to receive it. Imagine how the person worked for whatever it was and dreamed of having it, and the scene when he or she did not get it.
   Write a story like *Pig Money* using your own outline.
2 Imagine that Ianthe, or somebody else, after being disappointed at not getting what she had worked for, does something in keeping with her character which brings her a much greater reward from somebody.
   Write the story of how it happened and give it a good title.
3 Narrate a story in the first person singular (that is, using *I*) in which some unfair treatment is shown to a person and the person does something which causes a lot more trouble for everybody. Do not write *summary*. Describe the scenes to make your readers see them happening as in a film.

14 THE SCHOLARSHIP
Monica Skeete

Tuning in

Did you ever have to sit an examination to try to win a place in a school? Did your teacher coach you for the examination? Were you happy at school at that time? Here is a story imagined by a writer about how one little boy felt.

———

Sonny Boy lifted the lid of his desk cautiously and peered at the big ripe mango which was resting on his reading book. There was a great gnawing in his stomach as he had not eaten since lunch-time and it had been only split pea soup with two dumplings in it. That was
5 since 12.30 p.m. He wondered if he dared take two quick bites before Mr Callender returned from the toilet. He put out his hand to take it, then drew it away again. It was too big a risk he decided. The juice would be all over his fingers and, besides, Mr Callender would smell it. It was a quarter to five. He would wait until five, when he hoped
10 Mr Callender would let him go home.

He bit another piece from the pencil he was holding and his eyes wandered listlessly round the room and finally fastened on the open door before him from which Mr Callender's plump figure would emerge at any moment. He was writing an essay on 'Birds' and there
15 seemed so little he could say. He did not know many birds anyway. There was only the blackbird and the sparrow, and perhaps seagulls. Why couldn't Mr Callender give him a composition on something he knew about—crabbing, for instance? He could write pages about that. His mind was brought back abruptly to the present as Mr Callender
20 appeared.

'Finished yet? You don't have to take the whole evening to write one piece of composition.'

'Yes sir,' he said. He had only written six lines which were really only a list of the few birds he knew, and some like the nightingale and
25 the swallow that he had read about. It was better to get it over though. To wait longer was only to prolong the agony.

'Bring it here!'

He rose slowly and pushed back the chair with his right calf. It scraped harshly and tottered for a moment, before it crashed to the
30 floor.

'Put some life in you, boy. That's all you can do. This can liven you up, you know,' and he stretched out his hand towards the leather strap which remained either curled up like a lazy snake on his desk, or hung languorously from his shoulder. No one would suspect that there was such a deadly sting in its tail.

Sonny Boy picked up the chair smartly and walked with a sinking heart towards the head teacher. He handed him the exercise book half-closed. Mr Callender snatched it from his hand and glared at the few lines. Their smudged inkiness looked so pitifully inadequate against the vast expanse of white, unused paper.

'So that's how you waste my time! Think you can win a scholarship like that? Well, you go back and fill up that page, or else your back will know why not.'

Sonny Boy's lips trembled. His stomach was really folding up now and the wall clock pointed to five to five.

'I don't know anything about birds, sir,' he whispered, the front of his left canvas shoe rubbing on the laces of the right.

'Oh you don't? Well it is time you learnt.' He flung the exercise book back at him and walked towards a cupboard at the back of the room. He unlocked it and after a moment's fumbling, picked out a slim, red book. It was worm-eaten and he blew some fine dust from it before handing it to Sonny Boy.

'Read the first chapter of this and then make a summary of what you have read.'

Sonny Boy took the book in his inky fingers and, through tears, he read the title—*Birds of Western Europe*. He stumbled back to his desk and hastily wiped away a tear with the back of his hand. He was glad the other boys in his class were not here to see his weakness. He never cried, no matter how hard that strap flayed his seat. But now, he was so hungry.

It ended eventually. He had struggled through a maze of difficult words and had understood, only imperfectly, what it was all about. Still he managed to fill the rest of the page and his letters became noticeably larger as the composition lumbered towards its close.

'You may go now. Stay again after school tomorrow.' He suspected that Mr Callender let him go only because he himself was tired.

Sonny Boy leapt down the stairs two at a time as he dug his teeth into the mango. There was only one week left. He would be glad when this wretched scholarship exam was over. He had known no peace since he had been chosen with four others for special coaching. Every afternoon, at three-thirty, when the other children had gone, they had to remain behind to be subjected to a relentless drill in arithmetic and composition. There had been a gradual weeding out, and now only Sonny Boy remained to face the full blast of Mr Callender's erudition. Sometimes Mr Francis, the assistant teacher, took the lessons; then Sonny Boy enjoyed it. He made him write about exciting things, like carnival and spaceships. Mr Callender always grumbled afterwards that this scholarship exam was a serious

business and there was no time for such foolishness. Sonny Boy
80 would be twelve in November and this was his last chance.

It was not only Mr Callender who was after him. That is what made
it so bad. Ma and Nennen were just the same. Home used to be such a
happy place where he could do as he pleased. Now he could no longer
take his bag of cashew nuts and go next door to play 'jacks' with
85 Roland and Carl. He was forbidden to play cricket in the gap, or go
down to watch the boys tune the pans and beat steel band.

Usually it was nearly six o'clock by the time he came home
nowadays. Ma and Nennen would fuss around him and as soon as he
had eaten, they would light the big kerosene lamp, which was
90 normally used only when visitors came. He had to sit at the table and
do more sums from the arithmetic book which Mr Callender had told
Ma to buy. He liked arithmetic, but there was a limit to it. Sometimes,
to amuse himself, he would write little compositions about jets, or
cricket on the beach, but Ma always hovered anxiously over him and
95 she disapproved of his mere writing. Sums she could see and understand a little. They looked impressive on paper and she felt he was
really working when he was doing them. Sometimes he merely
copied out numbers on the book and wrote down imaginary answers.
She would pat him on the back fondly and say,
100 'That's right, me child. You get what I didn't get.'

He could not understand this concern. There was always an anxious
look in her eyes when she spoke about the scholarship. It hovered
about the house these days like a sinister spirit. Even the neighbours
regarded him as something special and frequent inquiries were made
105 about when 'it' was. Ma was always talking about how good education was and you could not get on without it. She was not educated, he
thought, and there was nothing wrong with her. As for Mr Callender!
He launched into long exhortations which Sonny Boy never really
heard. The one thing he understood was that he was expected to bring
110 credit to St Patrick's Boys' School, St Patrick's parish, and most of all
to Mr Callender himself.

Ma was fussing as usual. Sonny Boy stood stiff and clean from head to
toe. Ma had ironed his shirt a week in advance and it seemed to have
115 more starch than usual. His new shoes squeaked as he walked, and
they pinched his toes.

'You have your pen and pencil?' She pulled at his tie for the
umpteenth time.

'Yes, Ma.' He wondered how much longer his toes could stand this.
120 They had to walk down to the end of the gap to catch the bus. The
exam was held in town.

'I will carry the ink and the ruler.' Ma was wearing her best clothes
too—the white hat and dress she had bought last Christmas for the

church outing. Sonny Boy could tell that she was proud of him. She
held the ruler awkwardly, but in some vague way it shed a gleam of
academic glory over her. Many of the neighbours would be at the
standpipe. They would see her taking her son to sit the scholarship
exam. Sonny Boy wished he could do something about his feet.

'Ma, I could take off my shoes till I get to the bus?'

'What!' She turned on him so sharply that he almost fell over. 'Boy,
you must be mad! Come on. Walk fast. It must be nearly nine o'clock.
The sun getting high.'

She held his hand and pulled him along. They were late. The other
candidates had already taken their places. A lady was standing at the
door with a list in her hand.

'You are late. What name?'

'Sendall Thomas,' Ma answered nervously.

'Yes.' She ticked the name off on her list. 'Well, hurry along; on
your toes! The gentleman will show you where to sit.'

His stomach seemed to be contracting suddenly. He held out his
hand for the ink and ruler and Ma clung to his shoulder.

'God bless you, me child.' Her voice trembled, and he was not sure
that he did not want to remain out there with her, but the lady pushed
him forward impatiently.

'Hurry on!'

There must have been about three hundred boys and girls in the
large main room of the town hall. A gentleman who seemed to stand
at the other end of time beckoned him down the aisle. Like a robot he
progressed down the room. He did not know whether the beat of his
heart or the squeak of his shoes was the louder, but he reached the
shadowy beckoning figure at last. A hand moved up like a signpost
and pointed to a seat. Two boys had to stand up to let him pass in and
he bounced against his desk so that the ink spilled a little. However,
the arithmetic paper was in his hand at last.

They were not bad really. He had done sums like that dozens of
times and he had to write about cricket, so that was not so bad either.
He still could not see why Ma and Mr Callender made such a fuss.

They were out in the courtyard. Boys and girls from all over the
island milled about between mothers and schoolmasters. He spotted
Ma's hat and shouted.

'Ma!'

He bounded towards her and stopped short. There was Mr Callender. He too had come to be present at the kill.

'The papers were quite easy. You should do well,' he said. Sonny
Boy had never noticed him so relaxed before. He wanted to tell Ma all
about it but Mr Callender's presence overawed him. Before he could
say anything a bespectacled gentleman strutted up and thrust out his
hand.

'Hello, Callender! You here too? You country fellows are vying
with us these days. How many have you got?' He gave a swift scornful
glance at Sonny Boy whose shoes had begun to hurt again, and he was
fidgeting. He remembered now. That was Mr Tallboy, headmaster of
Colville School, the largest elementary school in town. His school got
nearly half of the sixteen government scholarships every year.

Ma had been ill at ease and she took the opportunity for them to slip
away.

Life was good again. For the next three weeks Sonny Boy could enjoy
cricket in the gap to his heart's content. He came to the house now,
panting and hugging a home-made bat under his arm. His shirt tail
flapped against his khaki shorts as he burst into the room. Nennen was
standing by the table and Ma was bending over a newspaper. He had
never seen her with one before.

'Me boy name in the paper,' she sobbed. Sonny Boy looked over
her shoulder. There was a spot of grease on a list of words where her
finger still rested.

At the top he saw his own name.

Talking about it

A *The events of the story*

1   *To prolong the agony* (l.26). What was the agony Sonny Boy was
    thinking about?
2   What do you understand by *At the top he saw his own name* (l.187)?
3   What was Sonny Boy prevented from doing until after the
    examination?
4   What was the risk Sonny Boy was afraid to take with Mr
    Callender?
5   What did Sonny Boy have to write the composition on for Mr
    Callender?
6   What did he prefer to write compositions on? Why?
7   What book did Mr Callender give Sonny Boy to read? How did
    Sonny Boy manage with it?
8   Which teacher was the better teacher, Mr Callender or Mr Francis?
    Why?
9   How did Sonny Boy's mother feel when she was going with him
    to the examination room?

110

B *Writing skills*

1 Which of these do you think the writer wants to say to you by means of the story (i.e., the *theme* of the story)?

   a)   it is always easy to pass an examination.

   b)   some teachers are bad teachers.

   c)   you have to go hungry sometimes to pass an examination.

2 Did the story have an ending you did not expect, or did it end as such stories usually end?

3 Did the story begin in a way that got you interested right away, or would you have preferred if the writer had given you a summary of facts to begin?

4 Who is the *narrator* of the story, Sonny Boy or someone outside like the author?

5 From whose *point of view*, that is, from inside of whom, is everything seen?

6 Does the writer want you to think that Mr Callender's compositions helped Sonny Boy in the examination, or not?

7 Here and there you are told little things to give you ideas about the three main characters in the story—Sonny Boy, Mr Callender and Sonny Boy's mother. Discuss whether any one of these is a *round* character.

8 The story has many words which are probably new to you. Does that make the *style* difficult for you to read or not?

9 What is *ironic* in the story, when you think about what Sonny Boy had to write about in the examination?

C *The use of words*

1 When you are writing your own stories or letters you need to use words that describe things in such a way that a person can imagine things as you see them in your own mind. Here are some words from *The Scholarship* which are very useful for that purpose. Look at how the writer used them and practise using them in oral sentences yourself.

cautiously (l.1)   *peered* (l.1)   *gnawing* (l.3)   *listlessly* (l.12)
tottered (l.29)   *languorously* (l.34)   *glared* (l.38)   *fumbling* (l.50)
stumbled (l.56)   *lumbered* (l.64)   *grumbled* (l.78)   *hovered* (l.94)
sinister (l.103)   *squeaked* (l.115)   *awkwardly* (l.125)
vague (l.125)   *gleam* (l.125)   *nervously* (l.137)   *clung* (l.141)
beckoned (l.148)   *strutted* (l.167)   *swift* (l.170)   *fidgeting* (l.172)
panting (l.180)

2   One of the words in each row below is somewhat alike or similar in meaning to the first word in italics. Look at how the first word is used in *The Scholarship* and discuss which other word in the row is alike in meaning.

dared (1.5)   bought   braved   opened
risk (1.7)   ruse   ridge   chance
wandered (1.12)   drifted   thought   wove
emerge (1.14)   pause   leave   revolve
prolong (1.26)   vote   lengthen   replace
agony (1.26)   ease   music   pain
harshly (1.29)   roughly   loudly   quickly
suspect (1.34)   believe   erect   enter
smudged (1.39)   oiled   smeared   printed
inadequate (1.39)   reversed   withdrawn   insufficient
vast (1.40)   pretty   smooth   huge
expanse (1.40)   outside   area   excess
hastily (1.57)   hurriedly   highly   recently
flayed (1.59)   flashed   wet   flogged
eventually (1.61)   finally   early   excitingly
struggled (1.61)   scattered   fought   selected
maze (1.61)   corn   estate   puzzle
noticeably (1.64)   conceitedly   clearly   properly
wretched (1.69)   unfortunate   stretched   repeated
relentless (1.72)   endless   small   incomplete
erudition (1.75)   knowledge   pride   ambition
normally (1.90)   definitely   orderly   usually
limit (1.92)   height   end   distance
disapproved (1.95)   disliked   disobeyed   directed
mere (1.95)   interesting   idle   only
impressive (1.96)   difficult   noticeable   stubborn
concern (1.101)   fuss   interest   conscience
inquiries (1.104)   tones   questions   replies
launched (1.108)   began   dined   comforted
exhortations (1.108)   advice   blessings   promises
credit (1.110)   permit   benefit   belief
glory (1.126)   strength   luxury   honour
contracting (1.140)   tightening   plotting   buying
impatiently (1.144)   noisily   angrily   restlessly
overawed (1.166)   afraid   above   alert
thrust (1.167)   use   push   belief

Beaming out

You might be interested in working on one of these ideas this week to make an addition to your work in your folder.

1 Read the part of the story telling about the day of the examination that Sonny Boy had to sit, and think about a day when you had to sit an examination too.

Then write the story of that day in your life—everything that happened, as far as you can remember, and what you did and felt. Give your story a title.

2 Imagine a girl who failed an examination. Make up an *outline* (see page 57) of a story to tell of things that happened to her in school and at home before the day of the examination, and after the examination results came out.

When you have your outline planned, write the story with the girl as the narrator in it to make a reader see it as if it is happening in real life: Give it a title afterwards.

3 Make up a story about a person who wanted to prepare himself or herself for an examination that was not far away, but who also wanted to spend all the time enjoying himself or herself with friends, looking at television, and so on.

Think of an ending for the story that would be easily believable because of what you put into the story before. Then write your story as *scene* as much as possible and give it an interesting title when you have finished.

15 A PRICE TO PAY
Timothy Callender

Tuning in

Many of the programmes shown on television in most countries are
crime stories in which a detective is looking for someone who has
broken the law. The writers and directors of such programmes try to
make them as exciting and dramatic as possible. Consider whether
this story would make an interesting television film.

———

He started from sleep in terror—and leapt up from the ground. For
a moment he could not understand the noise, and he crouched
there in the shadows with the whites of his eyes large in the darkness.
Then he realised that the noise was the barking of dogs and the shouts
5 of the police. They knew where he was. The dragnet was closing in.
   He looked around with a growing panic and a bleak despair
knocking at his heart. He was in the shadow of the trees, but ahead of
him, where he had to run, the beach stretched long and deserted in the
starlight.
10   He could not remain in the shadows any longer, because if he did,
with the men and dogs closing in on him, there would be no possible
chance of escape.
   He stood up for a moment, and then began to run. His feet pounded
through the loose powdery sand. He was very tired, because he had
15 already run a long way and had had very little time to rest. Yet, there
was no question of stopping for, around him and coming closer all the
time, was the circle of capture, and conviction, and death.
   Now, to his left, he saw the first lights of the torches fingering
through the trees. He was running closer to the edge of the sea now
20 where the sand was firmer, and he doubled himself over and prayed
that the lights would miss him. The trees were intercepting their
search and, for the moment, he was safe. But now, to his right, where
the trees thinned out and disappeared he saw the dots of light wavering
from spot to spot, and he knew that they were coming up from ahead
25 of him also. Behind him, the barking of the dogs sounded even louder.
How far behind? Three or four hundred yards? He could not tell.
   The only opening was the sea. He thought of this with a sort of
surprise that he hadn't thought of it before. Still running, he turned his
head and saw the rocks, heard the seething of the water over the long
30 low platform of sharp coral stretching submerged out into the dark.

114

He hesitated, and as he did so, a torch, clearing the trees, stabbed the darkness over his head and fell upon him, etching him out clearly against the backdrop of the white sea. 'Stop,' a voice shouted, and he froze in the glare of the light.

Then he turned, leapt out of the light, and plunged headfirst under the water, straightening out as quickly so as to avoid disembowelling himself upon the ragged teeth of the reef. The waves surged around him and already his lungs were bursting and his ears were pounding, for he had been almost out of breath when he took the dive.

He came out of the water behind a rock which shielded him from the glare of the torches and this afforded him a little breathing space. Further out to sea he could discern a large cluster of bigger rocks, and he felt that if he could only reach them, he would be relatively safe. He was gauging the distance towards the rocks, when he heard voices, and he knew that the police were coming out into the sea, walking upon the platform of reef and, as he looked, light gleamed whitely on the water, and jerked around from rock to rock, trying to spot him.

He took a deep long breath and plunged under the water again. Scraping his knees every now and then, he slowly worked his way towards the cluster, averaging his progress by the number of strokes he made. He surfaced again, and a beam of light skimmed over the spot where he had just come up. It was now moving away from him. He dived again. And now he reached one of the rocks that formed the cluster. He reached out and grabbed a sharp jutting portion of it. The insweeping waves threw him against it and bruised his body, blooded his gripping hands, but he did not lose his hold. He remained there whilst fingers of light patterned their search upon the sea and the sky and the rocks, and he shivered from fright and fear that, after all, he might not be able to escape them.

Three thousand dollars, he thought. That was a lot of money. That was the price they'd set on his capture. A lot of people will be looking for me in the hope of getting that, he thought. Three thousand dollars!

He stiffened and looked up. Above the noise of the waves on the rock, he could distinguish men's voices. And now he could hear the scrabbling noise of someone clambering up on the rock. He drew in his breath and pressed his back against the jagged side of the rock, waiting, his eyes staring upward. The rock rose behind and above him as he gazed from its base upward to the top edge silhouetted against the dark blue of the sky. He saw a pair of heavy boots, black and sharp against the sky, descending. He held his breath more deeply and his fingers clawed upon the rock behind. There was a splash. The policeman had dropped upon the rock platform below, and staggered as he landed, the light of the torch dancing crazily around at the impact. And then . . . the torch dropped from his hand into the welter of the waves. The policeman was close to him, so close that he could touch him, but the torch was gone, and the policeman couldn't see in the overhanging darkness of the rock.

The policeman swore under his breath, then shouted 'Hi!'

'Hinds?' someone replied.

80   'Yeah. I loss my light, man.'

'You ain't see nothing?'

'Hell, I don't know where he could have gone. I thought I was in front of him. You think he gone back in the opposite direction?'

'He was running this way, man.'

85   'So the smart thing to do is to head the other way as soon as he get in the water . . .'

'You might be right. Hell, why I ain't think of that before?'

'Hold on. I coming up to you. This place dangerous man. A man could slip off one o' these rocks and drown easy, easy.'

90   'Well, come up and lewwe go. We going have to wait till morning. We can't do nothing more now.'

The policeman scrambled up. The voices receded. The sea pounded on the rock as before.

The man waited for a few moments. Then he walked gingerly along
95 the treacherous platform and slipped into the water. In the distance he could see faintly the retreating figures of the policemen. Under cover of the rocks, he headed for the shore. He swam warily, for the sharp teeth of the reef were not easy to avoid.

At last he reached the shore. The barking of the dogs had receded
100 into the distance, and he ran along now, all caution gone.

'I don't want to have nothing to do with it,' his brother said. 'That is your own business. It was only a matter of time before this sort of thing happen. You was a blasted thief all your life, Franklyn, and now you reaping the rewards.'

105   'All right, Joe, I is a thief, yes, but that isn't mean I is to get hang for a thing I didn't do . . . '

'You trying to say you ain't kill her? Man, read the papers. You should see what they saying 'bout you. You up to your neck in trouble this time.'

110   'But, Joe, you got to help me. Blood thicker than water. You can't let them get me for a thing I ain't done.'

'Look. You may as well stop saying that,' his brother said. 'Read this.' And he threw a newspaper over to the hunted man, who took it and scanned it with terror-haunted eyes.

115   The headline said KILLER FORDE STILL HUNTED BY POLICE.

It told the world that he had killed a woman and that he had no chance to condemn or save himself.

Franklyn crumpled the paper into a ball and threw it, in a sudden spasm of frustration, violence and fear, away from him.

116

'Everybody got Franklyn Forde class up as a murderer,' he groaned, 'and, Joe, I ain't do it. You believe me, Joe, ain't you?' His eyes searched his brother's face in hope, but Joe's eyes were cold and hard and his lips compressed.

'Listen, you fool,' Joe said, and suddenly his expression changed. Tears blurred his eyes and he wiped them away brusquely. 'We grow up together, and you know how we mother try her best. And you had to turn out so. Time and time again I tell you was to behave yourself, 'cause after all, you is my little brother. But no, you won't listen. And now you running away from a murder charge. And I ain't in no position to help you. The wife in the next room there sick. She sick bad bad. And I been seeing hell lately. The grocery bill over a hundred dollars now and the man say he ain't giving me no more credit. The children hungry. They gone school today without tasting a thing this morning. Look at the old house. Falling apart. I in enough trouble already, and now you can't find nowhere else but to run here. You want me to get you out o' the island. You only out to preserve your own life and you don't care what happen to me once you get 'way. The police can ketch me and lock me up, and it won't matter a dam to you.'

'That ain't true, I only axing for a break, Joe. You won't never have to worry 'bout me no more. And you got to understand it is a mistake. I ain't kill nobody. I ain't done nothing to die for.'

'You still lying?' Joe suddenly shouted. 'You insulting my sense with that stupid lie?'

'I ain't do it.' His voice was shrill with the need to be believed, to be believed if only for a moment. But his brother's face had resumed its former expression. It was like stone.

'I only went in the room to steal, I telling you. I search round and the woman sleeping on the bed. I ain't touch her. And then . . . I hear somebody else come in the room. The woman own husband. I had was to hide. And then he stab her. I watch him . . . bram, bram, just so . . . and she scream out and she husband run. I jump up and run to her. I pull out the knife was to see if I could save her, and the blood spatter all over my clothes . . . you never see so much blood . . . and then everybody rush in and hold me. I ain't know how I manage to get away. I tell you is the same man got the police hunting me that kill the woman.'

'Look, man, you want to get out this island?'

'Yes, yes, yes . . . '

'Why you don't tell your own brother the truth then?'

'I tell you I ain't kill nobody . . . '

His brother suddenly leaped up and struck him. He fell on to the floor. His brother leaned over him and slapped him back and forth across the face. 'Tell me the TRUTH, boy. I want to hear the TRUTH!'

'What I tell you is the truth, Joe.' he said trying to keep the panic out of his voice, the panic that kept hammering at his brain. 'I ain't kill no woman.'

His brother hit him again. And again. He opened his mouth to make another anguished protest, but he saw his brother's eyes, and the 170 denial froze on his lips.

'All right, Joe,' he sobbed. 'I killed her, only I didn't mean to. I kill her. You satisfied? You going give me a break?'

They walked along the beach, their eyes darting from side to side with the fear of discovery in their minds.

175 'How far the boat-shed is from here?' Franklyn asked.

His brother pointed to an iron-corrugated roof among the trees. 'Is here I keep my boat.'

'Other people does use it?'

'Nobody there now. They fishing. I only stay home 'cause Sheila so 180 sick. I wish I had the money to buy the medicine for her . . . '

'I sorry, man, I wish I had some to give you.'

'All these years you t'iefing and yet you poor like me.'

'Is life.'

'You even worse off now. You is a murderer too.'

185 Franklyn said nothing, but he was full of hurt when he saw his brother look at him that way.

Silence. And Joe was thinking again: suppose the police come to question me! After all, I am his brother, and the police will surely come. I don't want to get into serious trouble like that. And my wife, 190 perhaps dying, and my children starving.

And Franklyn was thinking: What sort of chance I got, with three thousand dollars on my head. Is a wonder nobody ain't recognize me so far . . .

'This is the shed,' Joe said at last. The boathouse was dark and 195 gloomy inside as they entered. 'The fishing boat there,' Joe said. 'It old, but it can get us where we going. Wait here now till I come back. I got to make sure everything clear.'

'O.K, Joe. Thanks for doing this for me.'

Joe didn't answer. He looked at Franklyn for a moment and shook 200 his head slowly. Then he walked out into the sunlight and down the beaten path that led to the village. After he was gone Franklyn shut the door securely and sat down to await his return.

Joe was gone a long time. When finally Franklyn heard a knock, he was relieved, but cautious. He waited until he heard Joe's voice call 205 'Franklyn!'

Franklyn unbolted the door.

And then they were upon him and he went down under a mass of uniforms and clubs, screaming and struggling, as they pinioned his arms and dragged him roughly to his feet.

0   He snarled like a wild animal, and over the heads of the police in the doorway he saw his brother, his brother who had betrayed him. And, as he strove to get to him, shrieking out curses, someone hit him across the mouth, and they dragged him out into the open, and towards the waiting van.

Talking about it

A   The events of the story

1   What is meant by *The dragnet was closing in* (1.5)?
2   What made Franklyn leap up from the ground in terror?
3   Why were the police looking for Franklyn?
4   What do you think saved him from being caught by the policeman when he was gripping the rock?
5   What unlawful things had he done before he was accused of murder?
6   Why did he think a lot of people would be looking for him?
7   When Franklyn said he killed the woman was he telling the truth?
8   How did he explain why he was holding the knife and had blood on his clothes?
9   Do you think Joe believed Franklyn had killed the woman?
10   Who brought Franklyn to the boatshed and left him to hide there?
11   Who brought the police to the boatshed where Franklyn was hiding?
12   What reason do you think Joe had for betraying his brother?

B   The writing skills

1   The story can be divided into three scenes. What are they?
2   What would you say the author did to make the story exciting and dramatic?
3   Did you notice that the story does not begin by telling you things about Franklyn but by showing you Franklyn in action?
    Why do you suppose the author did that?
4   What would you say is the *climax* of the story, where you know whether Franklyn will escape or not?
5   Which of these seems to be the *theme* of the story (what the writer is really saying about life)?

    a)   once a criminal, always a criminal;
    b)   wrongdoers cannot escape the law;
    c)   people would betray one another for money.

6   If you were a film director making a film of this story how would you deal with the account Franklyn gave of how the murder was committed?

119

7   The story is told by a *narrator* outside the story—the author's voice. Could it have been told by Franklyn's voice instead?

8   Do you see any *irony* or anything *ironic* in Joe's betrayal of Franklyn?

9   Do you think you can write a story in the *style* of this one?

C   *The use of words*

When you read stories you must pay attention to the words used by the writer to describe actions and things, and take note of them to use them yourself in your own stories.

1   Here are some words used by Timothy Callender in *A Price to Pay*. Use them in oral sentences of your own.

   terror (1.1)   *crouched* (1.2)   *panic* (1.6)   *glare* (1.34)
   gleamed (1.46)   *clambering* (1.65)   *caution* (1.100)   *shrill* (1.145)
   darting (1.173)   *shrieking* (1.212)

2   The words in italics were used in the story. In each row there is another word of nearly the same meaning as the one in italics. Which one is it?

   bleak (1.6)   serious   lonely   vocal
   despair (1.6)   fear   anger   hopelessness
   deserted (1.8)   abandoned   dry   extinct
   submerged (1.30)   sunk   forced   lessened
   hesitated (1.31)   stammered   emphasised   paused
   surged (1.37)   tailored   increased   dyed
   jagged (1.66)   uneven   musical   nimble
   receded (1.92)   shaven   defiled   retreated
   scanned (1.114)   glanced   searched   covered
   relatively (1.43)   familiarly   comparatively   exactly

3   These words from *A Price to Pay* can be used in the blank spaces in the paragraph below. Which word fits into each blank space?

   blurred (1.125)   *silhouetted* (1.68)   *intercepting* (1.21)
   brusquely (1.125)   *warily* (1.97)   *snarled* (1.210)   *pinioned* (1.208)

   The detective was set on _____ the killer before any escape was possible. For a while he could see the figure _____ against the sunset, but it became _____ as the light began to fade. He followed _____, taking care not to be seen. But suddenly his arms were _____ by some giant behind, and a voice _____ a warning in his ear. Then he was _____ pushed into a passageway.

4   Discuss which meaning given in Column B is to be matched with which word in Column A.

A	B
conviction (l.17)	a sudden uncontrollable tightening of muscles
seething (l.29)	
discern (l.42)	acted in a deceitful way
spasm (l.119)	disappointment at not being allowed to do something
frustration (l.119)	
betrayed (l.211)	a punishment by a court of law; also a belief
	see clearly with the eyes or mind
	boiling or bubbling over, or full of activity

Beaming out

Using *A Price to Pay* as an example, you might like to do one of these this week to put into your class anthology.

1   Make up a story of a police chase of a person being hunted for a crime. You see many of them on television.

Begin your story with action just as Timothy Callender did in *A Price to Pay*, and continue it with action, writing the whole episode as scene.

2   Write the story of an episode in which a person enters a house to steal, but something happens in the house that makes him or her change plans and decide to get out. But when he or she is leaving he/she is seen by someone with a revolver.

Write the details of everything that happened up to then, and continue the account putting your own ending to the episode.

3   Imagine being held with forty other people as a hostage in a building by a group of three men and two women who are demanding that the Government release certain persons from jail and give them ten million dollars or all the hostages will be killed.

Write the story of everything you imagine happened, from the time the terrorists made everybody prisoners to the end of the chapter.

4   Write a story telling what happened after Franklyn was arrested by the police.

5   Make up a scene in which the husband of the murdered woman in *A Price to Pay* commits the murder, and write the story of what happened.

16 THE EXCURSION
C. M. Hope

Tuning in

What would you do if someone dared you to do something risky or dangerous? What do you do when somebody teases you to get you to act in a certain way?

When the boy in this story was teased was there more to risk than just being laughed at? Read the story and see.

———

Up on the hill, the old man sat on a stone, quietly watching. His knees were drawn up so that he could press his chin into the cups of his hands. He was motionless except, when every little while he shifted his bare feet in the marl. Sometimes the wind fluffed the grey
5 cap on his head.

Now he was watching the sun settle rapidly in the west among beds of grey clouds that were lined with ribbons of purple and gold.

Not so very long ago, he thought, the evening was warm and clear. But it had spurted suddenly to its finish. Now the twilight was wafted
10 in. It quickly flickered, then flitted away apologetically. The old man saw all this. He thought: it's like a man's life, bright and gay, then it comes to a sudden end. There is little twilight. He watched the clouds as they formed ludicrous yet life-like patterns in the sky.

'So much like some people,' he mumbled, 'always hurrying to
15 change this then to change that, and then back again.'

Whenever the old man was angry he mumbled to himself. He was very angry this evening.

'Always moving about,' he mumbled, 'moving this, moving that, jest because of ah excursion.'
20 Ants rushed about; some scrambled ticklishly over his feet. He stamped them vigorously, causing flecks of marl to fly about.

'Excursion,' he grumbled, 'goin' heay, goin' theay. Don't touch this, don't touch that.'

'Cooking a damn lot of food and yuh can't eat it.'
25 '"No don't, that ain't fuh you."'

The old man leaned over a little to slap his feet noisily.

'Running heay runnin theay, keeping a lot of blasted noise, jest fuh what? An excursion.'

He shook his head derisively.
30 'Mek yuh sick.'

The old man shuffled his feet lazily through the marl, and his head dropped slovenly on his chest. His cap cast a darker shadow over his face. His bent body was a grotesque shape in the falling darkness.

He kept on mumbling inaudibly. A cool wind gently fluffed his cap.
35 Now it was darker. The lights had begun to come on all over the place. He could feel the coolness of night stealing to his very marrow and he was tired.

He was nearly asleep, but a shuffling little figure jerked him to consciousness. He recognised the little figure; it was his good-for-
40 nothing grand-nephew Paul.

Paul scraped tediously down the road, but he did not see his great-uncle, for a house hid him from view.

He was going to the pipe for water. A bucket hung, like some misshapen yet forgotten ornament, over his arm.
45 'Young vagabond, always keeping a lot of noise and causing a lot of trouble,' the old man mumbled.

He closed his eyes and let his body stoop back in its old stupor.

'Think I could get on like he when I was young?'

'Lazy young varmit,' the old man muttered to himself, 'he now
50 studying up some wickedness.'

But Paul was studying up no wickedness. As he scraped along, his small feet willing to trip him up and his body all but lost in his too big clothes, he dreamed, and thought.

Tomorrow was the church excursion. His aunt, an ardent member,
55 had taken him every year. Tomorrow she would take him again. So he dreams of the fine time he should have. He thinks of all the stories he will tell his friends when he returns.

The old man's interest has abated. That tiredness seeps back to bones and that dull coma drugs his soul. Then a figure coming
60 abruptly out of the darkness catches his eye. He strains forward a little to see who it is . . . It is another boy, a fat boy about Paul's age. The old man recognises him to be Clyde Barker coming from his music lessons. If only Paul could be like him, he thinks. Then he shakes his head woefully. He watches him catch up quickly on the loitering Paul.
65 'Decent boy,' the old man mumbles. 'He got a mind fuh heself, he ain't like Paul at all.'

And he shifts his body more comfortably on the stool.

There will be six buses, Paul is thinking, and he wants to be in the first.
70 He can almost see himself, meticulously clean. For once he does not mind being so clean. Rather he likes it. He can show off his new shoes, his new socks and pants, new shirt, everything new. He sees the envious stares of the less fortunate boys. He passes them with merely a 'Hey yuh'. He doesn't even care when they jeer at him because his
75 clothes are a little too big.

He sees images of himself swaggering.

He swaggered a little and the bucket grated insolently over his arm.

He sees images of himself strutting and grinning at his friends as he takes his seat in the bus.

80 He is happy because he is going to have a very good time. A lot of food to eat and nothing to do but play. No water to bring, no running to the shop, no watching his aunt's goods; only play and food.

He can feel the wind whistle in his ears as the buses tear along the road. The speedometer registers, thirty, forty, forty-five, fifty.

85 'Hey Paul.'

Paul cocked his head to look disdainfully at the intruder. He summoned as deep a voice as he could to say:

'Hello, Clyde.'

He went on as if no one was there.

90 'I hear Carl beat you in a race,' Clyde called after him. Paul did not deign to answer. The driver had just taken a corner on two wheels.

Clyde dragged along behind him. There was a simpering look on his face as he taunted.

'Carl beat you, you can't run no run.'

95 Paul was a trifle annoyed.

'Ah know ah can beat you,' was all he proffered.

'You beat who?' Clyde demanded.

'You nuh,' Paul replied simply.

The bucket clanged peevishly at his side.

100 The bus is just passing two empty lorries and a car in the middle of a hill.

'Send 'er, send 'er,' he can hear the excursionists shout.

'Bet you can't jump over that hole,' Clyde said.

Paul stared disdainfully at him and the ditch. Then he said scorn-
105 fully.

'That's something too?'

'You can't jump over it though.'

'Yuh make me laugh.'

'Well do it then.'

110 Paul thought of his clean pants as he looked at the muddy water. He saw a teasing look on Clyde's face.

'Dat ain't nothing,' he said.

'Well do it then,' Clyde replied.

Paul did not answer.

115 It was quite dark now. The old man could see the two boys as they stood in the white arc cast by the street lamp. Through the branches of the overhanging tree he could see a few stars. He inhaled deeply. Then he saw Paul unhook the bucket and place it carelessly by the pipe.

"Tis a true saying,' he muttered, 'that dis world full of willing
120 people. Some willing to work, others willing to idle. And dat boy is one of the ones always willing to idle.'

124

He watched Paul take a few steps across the road. His puny body doubled up as he whipped through the air, over the ditch. He landed on the other side. For a moment he grasped at thin air to steady himself. But he felt himself sink. Then he remembered. The rain had fallen only yesterday, and when the rain fell, the other side was as bad as a cesspool. For what seemed to him like minutes, but in reality was only a few seconds, he struggled on the treacherous ground. Then he rolled over into the sticky mud.

At the boy's jump the old man jerked forward. Now the boy's plight shocked him out of his depression. His anger for the boy fled as he was filled with a more potent anger at the joker. Now he pitied Paul as he saw him wade through the dirtied water. He jumped up, leaning heavily on a stick, and he became more angry as he saw the grin on Clyde's face.

Clyde had a head start and he knew Paul would never catch him. He saw Clyde come panting up the hill, and Paul, tired but game, trying to catch him. Then the old man did a strange thing; he tripped Clyde with his stick.

Paul was on him in a flash. His muddy hands formed a pattern on Clyde's face. His fist filled Clyde's mouth as he opened it to shout.

'Stop,' Clyde gurgled, then as the fist came out he bawled:

'Murder! Oh Lord, oh Lord.'

Paul pummelled him silently and swiftly.

'Oh Lord, oh Lord,' Clyde yelled.

'Stop he, stop he,' he besought.

Someone pulled Paul off his chest. Then his cries grew louder.

'Aie! Aie,' he screamed.

Paul was silent.

'You unfair boy, beating the little fellow,' admonished the lady who held him.

'Pau-a-all,' someone called, and Paul knew that it was his aunt. He knew too, if she saw him he would be in trouble.

'Pau-a-all,' and her shout came closer.

He tried to pull away from his captor. He wriggled and struggled in vain. His aunt pounced on him.

'But look at you!' she cried. 'Where dat bucket?'

Someone brought it for her and she hurried Paul unceremoniously towards home.

They turned out of the smooth tarred road into the rough tenantry gap. Paul stumbled as his aunt pushed him before her They came to one of the small grey shacks. She dragged him in. An oil lamp flickered weakly on the table. The shadows were deep where the old man sat in the corner.

'What happened wid he now?' he demanded.

'Jest look at he,' she said 'look at he, and in these clean clothes I give he only this evening.' And she began to beat him with the strap she had taken from the roof.

'You disgusting boy,' she told him as she fervently laid on the
170 blows.

Paul screamed in pain.

'Now take off the clothes and get to bed,' she ordered, 'and let me tell yuh, not a foot you ain't going tomorrow.'

Paul did not mind the beating. He was accustomed to such. As he
175 peeled out of his clothes he sobbed with disappointment rather than anger. He wished that something would come to wipe them all off the face of the earth.

It was very late when his aunt finished washing his clothes. She was trying to iron them now.

180 'That boy going kill you,' the old man warned from the corner.

She looked at the boy and smiled.

The old man saw her smile and said: 'He so small and still kin beat all the rest of boys.'

She clamped the iron loudly on the table.

185 The old man sucked his teeth and said nothing more. He sat quietly and let her work silently. At last he said:

'You going let him go to the excursion though?'

'And who I going leave he home wid?' said the woman contemptuously.

190 Paul turned over on the bed and smiled.

Talking about it

A *The events of the story*

1 Why was Paul going down the road?
2 What was he dreaming about as he walked down the road?
3 *He sees images of himself strutting and grinning at his friends as he takes his seat in the bus* (l.78). When did he see that?
4 What does *puny* (1.122) tell you about Paul?
5 Why did he try to jump over the hole?
6 What happened when he jumped across the hole?
7 What did Paul do to Clyde?
8 What did Paul's aunt do to him, and why?
9 *She looked at the boy and smiled* (1.181) Why did she smile?
10 *. . . and let me tell yuh, not a foot you ain't going tomorrow* (1.172). Did Paul's aunt mean what she said?
11 Why did Paul turn over on the bed and smile?

B   The writing skills

1   Has the author made the old man seem to be like any old person you know?
2   Is there anything in Paul's and Clyde's behaviour that you would not have expected to happen?
3   Are you convinced about the reasons why the excursion was important to Paul?
4   Does the story have a surprise ending or not?
5   Is the story narrated from inside the old man, inside Paul, or outside both of them?
6   Do you think it was necessary to have the old man in the story?
7   Which of these, if any, do you think the author made up the story to say?

a)   when you disobey rules you will be punished
b)   old people do not understand what young people want
c)   people can find reasons for breaking their own rules

8   What reason do you think the author had for having the characters speaking in dialect?
9   Would you say the descriptive touches, like the description of the sunset, are overdone or out of place or do you think they help to make the story interesting?

C   The use of words

You will be able to describe things better if you know the words to use. So when you read stories you must try to learn to use the words which writers find useful.

1   What do the words in this group have in common?

shuffled (1.31)   *loitering* (1.64)   *swaggering* (1.76)   *strutting* (1.78)

2   What do the words in this group have in common?
muttered (1.49)   *mumbled* (1.46)   *jeer* (1.74)   *demanded* (1.97)
gurgled (1.142)   *admonished* (1.150)   *besought* (1.146)
simpering (1.92)

3   What do the words in this group have in common?

disdainfully (1.104)   *contemptuously* (1.188)   *scornfully* (1.104)
derisively (1.29)

4   Here are some very useful words that the writer of *The Excursion* used. Practise using them in oral sentences of your own.

wafted (1.9)   *flickered* (1.10)   *flitted* (1.10)   *vigorously* (1.21)

slovenly (1.32)   *stupor* (1.47)   *ardent* (1.54)   *seeps* (1.58)
intruder (1.86)   *taunted* (1.93)

5   In each row below there is a word which is somewhat similar in
    meaning to the first one in the row. Discuss the two words.

    a)   *motionless* (1.3)   empty   bare   still
    b)   *apologetically* (1.10)   regretfully   awkwardly   fancifully
    c)   *grotesque* (1.33)   adult   ugly   dead
    d)   *misshapen* (1.44)   lost   twisted   mistaken
    e)   *abated* (1.58)   lessened   bought   disposed
    f)   *coma* (1.59)   puzzle   sleep   bin
    g)   *abruptly* (1.60)   sadly   earthly   suddenly
    h)   *insolently* (1.77)   openly   actively   rudely
    i)   *treacherous* (1.128)   shocking   deceitful   sweet
    j)   *plight* (1.131)   state   height   opinion

Beaming out

Use your own experiences to do one of these in your spare time this
week and add it to those in your folder.

But it is time for you and your classmates to be putting out your first
anthology of stories. The class should elect two or three of you to
collect one story from each person and make arrangements for putting
them together with an attractive cover. Then put the anthology in the
library or anywhere that makes it easy for others to read.

1   Recall an occasion when someone dared you or someone else to do
    something—or you dared someone.
        With that memory in mind make up a story in which a boy or
    girl gets into trouble and out of it when he or she was teased one
    day about not being able to do something.
2   Paul was imaginging how he was going to enjoy the excursion. If
    you have ever gone on an excursion like the one Paul was thinking
    about try to remember the things that happened on that occasion.
        Then make up a story about an excursion which a little girl went
    on one day and which almost ended in disaster.
3   Imagine an old woman sitting on a chair on a verandah or near a
    window looking at the rain falling. Write a sentence like this: *Near
    the window the old woman sat on a chair quietly looking at the rain
    falling.*
        Then continue and tell a story that you imagine could have
    happened at that time.

17 AUNT SUZIE'S ROOSTER
Flora Squires

Tuning in

Perhaps you have come across a rooster or cock that behaved like the one in this story. And perhaps, like Beulah in the story, you regarded him as an annoyance. But Beulah's victory and relief did not seem to solve her problem.

(You probably know that in the West Indies a *duppy* means a ghost. A *gourmet* [say goomay] is a person who knows about the best meals, wines, etc.)

———

Beulah is undeniably a good cook. As a matter of fact she often turns out meals that can be only classified as a gourmet's delight. Beulah, however, cannot keep a job, and all because she will not prepare poultry in any form. She has acquired a definite allergy to
5 feathered stock, and it all began with Aunt Suzie's rooster, George. But I had better start at the very beginning.

Aunt Suzie, my maiden aunt, lived alone. Beulah performed the duties of cook and maid and Blenman did the chores in the yard.

George considered himself part of the family and the kitchen part of
10 his domain; at various intervals during the day he would visit the kitchen and, standing at the door, would tilt his head to one side and stare balefully at Beulah and when he was sure he had caught her eye, would solemnly wink and strut into the kitchen.

'Look, get!' Beulah would invariably say, and George would
15 promptly strut further into the kitchen. She took to throwing things at him, and he in turn became adept at dodging these missiles.

Sometimes when George was visiting the kitchen for the third or fourth time any day she would repeat, 'One of these good days I going to have to pay the Mistress for you, because I going lick you down
20 dead, dead. All the same, I going see to it that none of me hard-earn money going to pay for you. I never hear 'bout a good-for-nothing fowl-cock dat does defy human being like you.'

George would appear to be listening attentively, supporting himself on one foot, the other drawn up in anticipation of the next step he
25 would take. When Beulah had finished expressing her opinion he would drop the foot and continue his course, jump on to a table or cupboard and snatch some little tit-bit, fly to the kitchen door, usually followed by a wet sponge or whatever missile Beulah had managed to throw after him.

30 Thus it continued despite Beulah's complaints to Aunt Suzie.

One day, however, George went too far. Aunt Suzie had baked and iced a cake for tea—the parson was coming. His visits were a bright spot in Aunt Suzie's life as she considered him such a delightful fellow, so attentive and always eager to share her joys and her sorrows.

35 George walked into the empty kitchen, jumped on a table, spied the cake on the top of the stove, and was soon <u>gorging</u> himself with generous pecks of the icing; he had picked all off the top of the cake and had started on the sides, when Aunt Suzie returned to the kitchen.

'Sush, scat,' she cried and made a grab at him, but with a squawk, 40 George eluded her grasp and flew out of the kitchen leaving a wrathful Aunt Suzie with a few brown feathers in her grasp.

Hearing the commotion, Beulah and Blenman, who were in the yard, rushed into the kitchen. 'What happen, Mistress?' inquired Beulah, and before she could be answered, she spied the ruined cake. 45 ''C'' dear,' she said. 'Looka dis thing! Mistress, what I tell you? I tell you George ain't no good. I tell you to get rid of he long ago.'

George had by now returned to the scene of the crime. He stood, unabashed, at the door, feathers unruffled and cocked his head as was his wont.

50 'Look he there!' shouted Blenman making a vain attempt to grab him.

'Mistress what you going to do? You going let George get way with dis thing? He ain't getting no better, every day he t'iefing more and more, and it now reach the stage that you can't put down nothing in 55 peace.'

'Yes,' agreed Aunt Suzie sorrowfully, 'I think he has gone too far. We shall have him for dinner on Sunday.'

Beulah's eyes shone with glee. 'Bake he, or stew he, Mistress?'

Aunt Suzie said, 'I think it will be better to have him in stew; he is 60 old and must be tough.'

Eagerly Beulah offered, 'I going give you a nice, thick, brown gravy, with English potatoes, carrots and plenty onions. I will put he on early to cook; all the same, if I find he too tough, I will put some green paw-paw in the pot to soften he up.'

65 Suddenly Beulah spotted George again at the door. Shaking her forefinger in his direction she said, 'George, I know I was going ketch up with you! When you done cook on Sunday, it going give me great pleasure to crunch you neckbone between me teeth.'

On Saturday evening Beulah and Blenman chased the cock around 70 the yard. He tried his best to outrun them, and the hens clucked and cackled their encouragement to him, but at last he was cornered. As Beulah lifted him, she said, 'I thought you did heavier, with all the t'iefing you does do. Like you ain't even put on no weight. I hear the old people say, ''What don't kill does fatten,'' but you ain't prove that 75 at all.'

On Sunday Aunt Suzie could not bring herself to eat George, and so Beulah and Blenman did justice to the meal, and as they became replete, commented on the fact that George had proved to be very juicy and tender, despite his age. Thus did it seem that George had met an ignominious death.

The following day, everything was so quiet in the kitchen that Beulah had to admit to Blenman that she missed George and her daily skirmishes with him.

On Wednesday morning Beulah was preparing the midday meal when she heard a familiar flapping of wings, and turning around was flabbergasted to see George snatching a piece of potato from the table. Her mouth dropped open in disbelief. There was dead silence. Then she screamed.

Both Aunt Suzie and Blenman ran into the kitchen where they found a hysterical Beulah. When they had managed to soothe her to some extent, Aunt Suzie inquired what had happened.

'George duppy,' she gasped.

'George's what?' asked Aunt Suzie in disbelief.

'George's duppy. I just see he.'

'Beulah,' exclaimed Aunt Suzie, 'what on earth are you talking about?'

'Mistress,' said Beulah, 'I see George duppy wid my own two eye. He jump up 'pon the table, snatch up a piece of potato, and fly through the door just like he used to do when he did living.'

'Rubbish!' snorted Aunt Suzie.

'Mistress,' said Blenman, his eyes wide with amazement, 'I see he too. I sure I see something brown fly past me in the yard.'

'Rubbish!' insisted Aunt Suzie.

At this stage, George appeared at the door.

'Looka he there!' cried Blenman, his eyes almost popping from their sockets. Three pairs of eyes stared at the apparition.

'Yes, it's George!' exclaimed Aunt Suzie. 'Then whose cock did you kill on Saturday?'

'Mistress, I swear it did George.' Beulah's feet refused to bear her weight any longer, and she collapsed into the nearest chair.

'Yes, Mistress,' Blenman said definitely. 'It was George. I help to ketch he.'

But Aunt Suzie replied: 'It was George at the door just now, there is no doubt about it, so obviously another cock was killed. It might have looked like George, and as I have only one Rhode Island cock, you took it for granted that it was George. Do you remember you remarked on its lack of weight, and on how tender it was? I wonder where the cock that was killed came from?'

Beulah rose shakily to her feet.

'Mistress, regardless of what you say, I still know George dead. I help to eat he, and this is he spirit now come back.'

George continued to pay daily visits to the kitchen and continued his pilfering, but Beulah pretended that she did not see him.

125   On Saturday when Aunt Suzie paid Beulah her week's wages the latter said: 'Mistress, I likes you, I respects you, and I likes working for you, but I just got to leave. I can't stand it 'pon a day when that fowl-cock duppy come and stand by the door and wink he eye at me. It is more than a body can stand.'

130   Despite Aunt Suzie's pleadings, Beulah left.

    The following Sunday, Aunt Suzie, as was customary wended her way through the congregation exchanging greetings. Mrs Batson, however, turned her back on her and ignored her salutations. Aunt Suzie was puzzled, but nevertheless, she shrugged her shoulders and 135 continued chatting with other neighbours.

    It was Blenman who, on the next day, threw light on Mrs Batson's lack of courtesy.

    'Mistress,' he said, 'you know who fowl-cock we kill? It was Miss Batson own. Her cook tell me that Miss Batson did buy it and it get 140 way the same day.'

    'Oh dear,' exclaimed Aunt Suzie. 'How awful! I must offer to get her another one.' She paused and then said contemplatively, 'I would give anything to know where George was when the other cock was being killed.'

145   From behind her came the flapping of wings. Looking around, she saw George standing poised on one leg in the doorway. 'Where were you that day, you rascal?' she demanded. Regarding her steadily, Aunt Suzie's rooster solemnly (and was it with a touch of malicious humour, she wondered) slowly winked his left eye at her and crowed.

Talking about it

A   *The events of the story*

1   Who or what was George?
2   What did Beulah do in Aunt Suzie's household?
3   What sort of pilfering did George do sometimes?
4   How did the rooster behave like a human being?
5   What made Aunt Suzie agree to have him for dinner?
6   What did Beulah and Blenman notice about the rooster they had for dinner on that Sunday?
7   Why did Beulah become hysterical on Wednesday morning?
8   Why did Beulah leave Aunt Suzie's household?
9   Why did Miss Batson treat Aunt Suzie with discourtesy?

10 What explains how Beulah and Blenman came to make a mistake when they caught the rooster?

B The writing skills

1 Which of these, if any, would you say the writer wanted to do in writing the story in that way?

a) annoy the reader
b) amuse the reader
c) excite the reader
d) sadden the reader

2 How did the writer make it easy for you to believe how the wrong rooster was caught?
3 Would you say that George is a character in the story or not?
4 What characteristics did the writer give to George?
5 Compare how Aunt Suzie spoke with how Beulah spoke. Was the writer right to have them speaking differently?
6 The *plot* of a story is the way things hang together with one thing depending on another, one thing causing another, and so on. Does the plot of this story depend on a coincidence that is unlikely to happen?
7 What is amusing about any of these?

a) *would solemnly wink and strut into the kitchen* (1.13)
b) *usually followed by a wet sponge* (1.28)
c) *the hens clucked and cackled their encouragement to him* (1.70)
d) *Beulah's feet refused to bear her weight any longer* (1.109)

C The use of words

People learn to use the words of a language by observing how persons who know the language use them, and then by trying to use them too.

1 Look back at where and how each of these words is used—the context of the word—and then try to use it in a sentence of your own:

strut (1.13)   *missiles* (1.16)   *eluded* (1.40)   *commotion* (1.42)
commented (1.78)   *flabbergasted* (1.86)   *hysterical* (1.90)
snorted (1.100)   *collapsed* (1.110)

2   Discuss what the second word of each pair here could mean.

class = group
classified =

anticipate = act before the time
anticipation =

obvious = clear
obviously =

contemplate = look at with
                          thought
contemplatively =

baleful = threatening
balefully =

custom = usual manner
customary =

3   From the way in which each of the words in List A is used in the
    story discuss which word in List B has a similar meaning.

A   *domain* (l.10)   *adept* (l.16)   *gorging* (l.36)   *generous* (l.37)
    unabashed (l.48)   *unruffled* (l.48)   *glee* (l.58)
    skirmishes (l.83)   *wended* (l.131)   poised (l.146)
B   unashamed   skilful   balanced   joy   went   territory
    plentiful   stuffing   calm   fights

Beaming out

Here are some ideas for you to do your own thing. You might wish to
use one of them or one you can think of for yourself to work on this
week.

1   Think of a puppy you have observed and imagine someone who
    has always been annoyed by what the puppy did. Then think of
    something that was done (make it up) to get rid of the puppy or to
    get away from it. Then imagine the return of the puppy and what
    happened then. Try to see everything from an amusing point of
    view.
        Perhaps you could name the puppy *Rusty* and end your story
    with this sentence or a sentence like it.
        *Rusty turned, cocked his little tail up into air, twisted his head to one
    side, and then with his left hind foot kicked some dirt up into the air.*
2   Write the story of a scene in which a cat of a clergyman follows the
    gardener around as he tends the garden, but the gardener is afraid
    of cats and does this and that to scare the cat away, but the cat
    merely looks at him with steady eyes. From time to time the
    gardener steps on the rake, falls over the barrow, knocks over a
    potted plant, pricks his finger, and so on, because the cat is always
    near. The gardener is convinced that the cat is causing things to
    happen to him. When the clergyman comes into the garden the
    gardener complains about the cat, and as he is doing so he steps
    into a hole and sprains his ankle. The cat runs off.

3   See if you can make up a story with your own plot in which some
     of these words and phrases could be used:

*domain   balefully   the scene of the crime   solemnly   strut
gorging   threw light on   promptly   defy   did justice to   eluded
commotion   as was customary   glee   unabashed   unruffled
a touch of malicious humour   skirmishes   flabbergasted   hysterical
snorted   amazement   collapsed   pleading   wended*

18 FLY BACK TO ME
A. N. Forde

Tuning in

A catapult, you might know, is also called a slingshot, and you know some boys use it to shoot birds, taking joy in killing beautiful creatures. Do you know any boy who felt sorry about using a catapult?

In this story a boy with a catapult learns a lesson. Read the story and see how.

———

Jerry opened the door of the pigeon loft. The pigeons came flocking out into the cool morning. They were greedy for their feed.

They flew crazily in the air waiting for him to throw the feed upon the ground. Jerry flung his hand in a careless arc and let the broken scrap corn fall through his fingers. From all angles they came towards the corn, slapping him unwarily with their wings.

But Jerry was not happy this morning.

Two days had passed since his best pigeon had disappeared. He had called it Wonder after the name of an aeroplane he had seen in a *Boy's Own Magazine*. Yes, Wonder had disappeared.

Jerry looked up into the sky more from habit than anything else. A small school of gauldings were soaring high over his head.

But there was no sign of Wonder.

He had never realised before how much this pigeon meant to him. He hadn't reared it. It was really a stranger that had arrived months ago out of the blue. Since then it came and went, day after day, and had become a fixture as casual as the rise and set of the sun. He had taken a fancy to it and accepted it as theirs—his and his mother's. Strangely enough his mother liked it too—and she usually hated the sight of any pigeon trespassing in her yard. But with Wonder it was different. You couldn't help liking that pigeon.

It was a beautiful pigeon. The most delicate shades of green, blue and fawn, bright and dull, blended on its breast; and when it shook its head the colours on neck and wings merged in a delightful shifting harmony. Its tail was black and white like a draught-board in pattern and its feet were a fragile pink.

Jerry looked back up into the sky. A few scattered pieces of corn still lay on the ground, exciting the eager contention of the pigeons. The gaudlings were out of sight, but there was still no sign of Wonder.

Two days! Perhaps he might never see it again!

His heart felt heavy and the chucklings of the pigeons near him went

137

unnoticed. He hardly thought of them today; and when his mother called, he answered listlessly.

'Yes, Mom.'

35 'Wonder come?'

'No, Mom.'

'Where he could be?'

'I doan' know, Mom.'

Perhaps it had died, he thought. Or had been killed!

40 Then his mother spoke again:

'I bet you anyt'ing one of them boys hit it with a catapult. That is why I always stop you from using one. You all does kill people's chicken and things just for fun. I will brek your hand if I see yo' with one.'

45 Jerry did not answer. He could not. He felt uneasy. For he had a catapult—though his mother did not know it. He had made it himself with his scout knife and was very proud of it. Its edges were smooth and well-turned. And the fork tapered neatly down into the stem. He had made it shine with some stolen varnish, and the clean red rubber

50 which he had got by swapping the face of a watch for it was tied with thin wire to the branches of the fork. He had made the catapult in moments of quiet, always out of sight of his mother.

Two days ago he had had his first hit with the catapult, had drawn his first blood.

55 He remembered it as if it were now. The head and upper breast of the dove peeping out over the house-top. The challenge it presented. His trembling eagerness to try his luck. The catapult sticking in his pocket and giving him trouble to get it out. The 'heffing' of the weapon when he raised it for the shot. The breathless ecstasy of taking

60 aim. The suspended moment. And then he had loosed the tight straining length of rubber and the stone flew from the sling.

The bird toppled over backwards out of sight.

He stood stunned with the rapture of it all, unable to gather his thoughts together. He was a hero. But he must get the bird, he said to

65 himself. He wanted to run around into the person's yard and ask if he could climb the house and take it off the roof. But he dared not. His mother would hear of it and he was sure to get a 'cussing.' He stifled his eagerness to see the dead bird and went on home, carrying the keen satisfaction of a deed well done. Now he could speak with authority.

70 This was the first of many—perhaps he would become a better bird-catcher than any other boy in the district. At least, he had shown his mastery. He had made the grade.

But he should have got the bird as testimony. Those boys were sure to question and suspect something shady if they didn't see the bird

75 themselves. He could almost hear Dan's sarcastic laugh:

'Who yo' think yo' can fool? Ha! Ha! Ha! With your mother

watching every step you make, what bird you can shoot?'

And whatever Dan said was sure to be echoed by his pals.

Still, he knew he had shot it. What more? And with the freshness of
triumph in his heart he had walked lightly home. He was just in time
to hear his mother calling him loudly to feed the pigeons. He fed them
but, surprisingly, Wonder had not turned up. He found it strange but
it was not till evening that he begun to think seriously about Wonder's
absence. Where was the pigeon?

Suppose he had killed it!

The next day came and the absence of the bird became more
perplexing.

And two days had now passed.

Yes, it was quite possible. He wasn't sure it was a dove he had shot.
It might have been a pigeon for that matter. And why not Wonder?
And the irony of it! His first catapult, his first shot, his first bird had
deprived him of the creature dearest to him. What a nasty thing to
happen.

He moved away from the pigeon roost meditatively. Almost in a
trance he heard the pigeons suddenly rush out of the loft and knew by
the whirring sound that they were wheeling in the air above. They
didn't feel like him, he thought. Without interest, he turned and
followed them with slow eyes as they circled above.

And then he saw it! There could be no doubt about it!

Moving slowly from the upper air, a pigeon was coming down to
earth. Instinctively he knew. It was Wonder.

His eyes clung to the small moving creature.

It seemed in danger of toppling over into space and one wing was
paddling inexpertly, but there was greatness in the way it came—like
a torn fishing vessel limping into harbour.

Jerry stood and watched, amazed and heartened in the same breath.
He felt the pressure of a new joy rising inside him and he shouted with
all his might!

'Mom, here it is!'

The bird descended slowly—majestically, and the other pigeons
flew restlessly about it. It was sheer joy to watch the act. They flew
around and before like excited guards of honour, and the bird at last
landed safely at Jerry's feet. He stood and looked down at it, not yet
sure of himself, not quite sure what to do with the joy in his heart.

Then in a childish but masterful impulse he took something from
his pocket in haste and broke it in two. It fell a yard or two from the
bird.

When his mother ran out, Jerry was fondling the fluttering bird and
at his feet was a smooth, well-polished, but now useless catapult.

Talking about it

A *The events of the story*

1 Who or what was Wonder?
2 Why was Jerry not happy that morning?
3 Why was he proud of his catapult?
4 Why did he keep it out of sight of his mother?
5 What did he shoot with his first shot from his catapult?
6 What did he afterwards think he had done with his catapult?
7 Why did the pigeons *suddenly rush out of the loft* (1.95)
8 What was wrong with Wonder when he came back? How do you
   suppose it happened?
9 What did Jerry break in two, and why?

B *The writing skills*

1 What would you say is the point or theme of the story, the
   meaning the writer wants a reader to get?
2 The story begins with Jerry about to feed the pigeons. Then there
   is what is called a *flashback* to what happened before. Then we are
   brought back to the present with Jerry and the pigeons in the yard.
   Where exactly does the *flashback* begin and end?
3 *And the irony of it!* thinks Johnny (1.91). What did he see as *irony*, or
   as being ironical?
4 The *climax* of a story is that point in the story when you know that
   the whole matter or problem or question is at last decided one way
   or the other. What do you think is the *climax* in this story?
5 A story is usually about some person (or animal) having a
   problem. The person has a problem and a *conflict* with another
   person or persons (like Franklyn in *A Price to Pay*), or with the
   forces of nature (like a person caught in a hurricane), or with
   himself (like Kenneth in *The Valley of Cocoa*). In *Fly Back to Me*
   which kind of conflict is there?
6 Remember *sentimentality* is having more than the right amount of
   feeling about something, or having a strong feeling about
   something which does not deserve that feeling. Would you say
   there is sentimentality in this story or in the author's attitude?
7 The point of this story depends on a *coincidence* or accident: if
   Wonder had not disappeared *at the same time* that Jerry used his
   catapult, Jerry's conscience would not have bothered him—he
   would not have felt guilty. But a coincidence or accident like that
   usually makes a story unconvincing—hard to believe that it really
   happened that way—because that hardly happens in real life.
   Sometimes, however, the author puts in things that cover up that

weakness in his story and we find ourselves believing it.

Did the writer succeed in making this story convincing, in spite of the coincidence?

C   *The use of words*

1   Discuss which of these words best fits in each sentence below:

eager (1.28)   *ecstasy* (1.59)   *sarcastic* (1.75)   *echoed* (1.78)
perplexing (1.87)   *trance* (1.95)

a)   In a very _____ tone I told her she was a kind person.
b)   We were all so _____ to help that we caused confusion.
c)   I find it very _____ to understand why they treated him so.
d)   Sometimes I get a feeling of _____ when I listen to beautiful music.
e)   All of her friends just _____ what she said, instead of correcting her.
f)   I thought he was in a _____ because his mind was so far away.

2   Discuss which word in list A can be paired with a word in list B that is near to it in meaning.
A   *unwarily* (1.6)   *blended* (1.23)   *merged* (1.24)
      suspended (1.60)   *testimony* (1.73)   *triumph* (1.80)
B   victory   mixed   hung   evidence   carelessly   joined

3   Discuss how each of these words should be used in sentences.

soaring (1.12)   *fragile* (1.26)   *listlessly* (1.33)   *uneasy* (1.45)
stunned (1.63)   *rapture* (1.63)   *meditatively* (1.94)   *restlessly* (1.111)

Beaming out

Perhaps the easiest kind of story to make up and write convincingly is one in which a person is having a problem or conflict with the forces of nature; and the most difficult kind might be that in which a person has a problem or conflict inside himself or herself. In between probably comes the kind in which a person has a problem or conflict with another person or persons.

Try to make up a story of one of these three kinds this week. You may use an idea suggested here, if you wish.

1   There have been heavy rains. The river near Krishna's house is rising rapidly. A dangerous flood is threatening.

Make up the story of Krishna's battle to save himself, his family, his house, and so on.

2 Sheila has a beautiful puppy, Spot, that has not yet learnt where home is and that wanders elsewhere sometimes. One day Spot is missing, and when Sheila goes looking for him she sees a girl named Jackie with a puppy like Spot.

Make up the story of the scenes in which Sheila missed Spot, how she was looking for him, how she saw Jackie and the puppy, and what happened afterwards.

3 Milton wants Sonia to be his friend but he thinks she prefers Clayton because Clayton can buy things to give everybody. Milton know he can take money from his father's stall in the market and behave like Clayton, but he does not want to be dishonest. One day Sonia asks him to prove he is not mean and stingy by giving her a present. What decision does he come to, and how?

Make up the scenes from the beginning where Milton tries to get Sonia to be his friend and she shows her preference for Clayton. Then continue the story to whatever end you want to give it, putting in a *flashback* if you find it useful or necessary.

19 THE BLACK DOG
Robert A. Lucas

Tuning in

Sometimes when a person is provoked over and over again there is no telling what might happen. Do you agree? Can you remember anyone being provoked over and over again and what he or she did? In this story a dog makes a man lose quite a lot besides his temper.

———

Whenever he saw the black dog he would stamp and curse. He hated it with a remorselessness with which he had never hated anything before. 'Get out, you beastly dog!' he would shout, and with its bob-tail—if it could be called a tail, for it was rather a stump in the
5 wrong place that made its bare hindquarters look vulgar, almost obscene—it would crawl lazily out of the yard, its bones moving plainly under its dirty, loose skin that resembled old patent leather. Its ears were too big and hung loosely down at the ends. Its face had the character of a heinously ugly man. Its eyes were oppressive, and its
10 long, partly toothless mouth always carried froth and dangled saliva from a colourless tongue. It also had a dirty and unsightly sore on its bare buttocks.

'Get out!' old John Brown would shout, throwing two stones after it. He always missed; that was the irritating thing about the black dog.
15 He had no idea from where it came and he termed the annoyance of this pest as a curse and a persecution of the devil. He could not by chance forget the eggs of his hens in the coop; the sly dog would undo the latch and carry them off one by one. He even saw it one day rushing his hens for their feed, and carry off a three-week-old chicken
20 without heed to the shouts and stones he flung behind it.

He made repeated attempts to poison it with cement mixed with Purina feed which he left purposely in the yard after dusk, but always next morning he would see it untouched. He tried rat poison on pieces of meat which disappeared repeatedly but the sly dog still existed.
25 One day he left four and a half pounds of salted fish to cure atop his coop which was five feet in height. He went into his garden to plant corn for half an hour. When he returned the tasty salted fish had disappeared into the gullet of the vagabond dog. The dog was cunning; he knew it. It hid behind the trunks of trees and between the
30 bushes about his garden, all day watching his movements with its sly, carnivorous eyes. It evaded with an incredible, irritating coolness the boulders he flung after it. He knew that it was poor nerves that made him miss, so he got a band of boys to help eradicate this persistent,

damaging pest—damaging because he was lately having heart attacks
35 and his doctor told him that he should not worry or fret. He knew that
the black dog was responsible and he vowed to get it.

After restless stoning by the band of boys for two months, he did
not see the villain and he believed that it had starved to death in the
bushes.

40 One day, while forking his garden, he heard one of his brooding
hens making a loud racket. He ran to the yard, thinking the cause was a
mongoose, but instead he was just in time to see the black dog grab a
chicken from the hen which was trying vainly to put up a fierce fight in
defence of her young ones.

45 His heart almost failed him. He flung his heavy fork with superhu-
man strength towards the dog but it fell short of its target. Quickly he
picked up big lumps of dirt and flung them with all his might at the
thieving black dog that had come back into his life.

He clenched his fists and shook them to the sky, swearing at the
50 creature as it bolted away.

With all precaution he locked up his stock and all things that the
black dog was capable of stealing, almost as if he was preparing for a
siege or an invasion.

He took out a shotgun from an old trunk that he had not used for
55 over two years; he loaded it and hung a large piece of meat on a clothes
line that ran across the yard, just the right height, so that the black dog
would leap for it, giving him a chance to blast it.

He sat ten paces away at the gable end of the house waiting. Night
came and he was still waiting. It was time for dinner. He was hungry,
60 mosquitoes bit him, he sweated with an ever-increasing suspense. Still
he waited and was determined to hold out.

Night drew on but there was no black dog. He stamped his feet, and
slammed his fists together with resolution. His house was in darkness,
the stars shone brightly and the full moon rose on the horizon. Alone
65 with resolution and immovable determination he sat on a log with the
gun on his lap, stifling disquieting and weary yawns.

Soon he forgot to slap the mosquitoes that bit him and he dozed off.
Suddenly he was awakened by a dangling of the wire from which the
meat hung. He opened his eyes quickly and saw the black dog darting
70 off with the meat. He opened fire. He loaded the shotgun and fired
again, but the dog was quickly out of range. He ran after it uselessly
for the cunning dog, that appeared so listless during the day, dwindled
swiftly to a far black dot among the beds of the garden.

His night was restless. The dog haunted him even in his sleep.
75 Before dawn he got out from bed, loaded his shotgun and carrying
ample cartridges with him sent on a wide search for the villainous dog.

He went far along his garden, he searched among ditches, in ravines
and among bamboo stools. The sun rose and became blazingly hot;

still he was on the hunt. About a mile from home he suddenly came upon a cottage with two cars parked before it and a group of people talking excitedly on the road. A man pointed at him with excitement and all heads turned to look at John Brown. He had come upon the scene from the back of the cottage after his long journey through deserted back lanes in his hunt for the dog. He had wanted to drop in at the cottages for a drink of water and a pause from the cruel heat of the sun, but instead he had stumbled upon two men who came down the back steps of the building carrying something that looked like a corpse on a stretcher. He did not understand the situation of the business, nor when the two attendants had looked at him with a surprise that he had partly taken for shock.

The old shotgun was held in his right hand. He shifted it to his left in an old hunter's action to procure a handkerchief to wipe his sweaty face and the salty sweat from his eyes.

The crowd at the roadside, spurred by his untimely movement, back away suddenly with precaution.

A detective drew his gun quickly. 'Drop it,' he said, 'drop the shotgun.'

Old John Brown dropped his shotgun stupidly. He wanted to ask what was the matter but his tongue was like a heavy dry leather.

The detective nodded towards his assistant who drew out a pair of handcuffs from his pocket. 'We were right when we said that murderers always visited a scene after their crime.'

'Look,' John Brown tried to defend himself, 'I was just hunting.'

'Now is no hunting season, man, you know that. You didn't find the treasure of the poor man, whom you murdered last night, so you came back to make a search. You did not expect the police would be notified so quickly about it, did you? Your mistake was in coming back with that gun in such a sneaky manner.'

'Look, what are you talking about, Chief?'

'Shaddup! Hell alone knows where you guys get the guts to blow a man's head off with a shotgun and have the mouth to talk back like that.' The detective dipped a hand into one of his pockets and withdrew an old tie which he dangled before him.

'Where did you get that?' old John Brown questioned.

'I though you would ask that. It's also what you came back for. You dropped it under the man's house last night. Perhaps the dog had scared you into dropping it or you tried to strangle the poor thing with it to keep it quiet.'

John Brown recognised the old tie as the one that he had used to tie the piece of meat to the clothes wire-line in his effort to entrap the black dog. The dog on snatching the meat had run away with the tie.

'You recognise the dog all right and it recognises you.' The heavy handcuffs clicked on his arms. 'That does it.'

He saw the black dog growling and staring at him fixedly with its ugly bloodshot eyes. It parted its crooked, discoloured teeth in a devilish snarl like a mocking grin.

'I will kill you!' John Brown shouted.

'You won't kill anyone any more, man. Get in the car.'

'It's a mistake, I tell you—it's a terrible mistake.'

'Shut up!'

The car pulled out. The black dog barked after it, then sat on its bare haunches and scratched its dirty ears, staring after the car.

Talking about it

A *The events of the story*

1   Why did the man hate the dog?
2   What did the man do in his first two attempts to kill the dog?
3   What made him get some boys to keep stoning it away?
4   What finally made him get his shotgun to shoot it?
5   What had happened at a cottage a mile away from his home?
6   What did the police think the man had done?
7   What was the clue that the police thought showed the man as the guilty one?
8   How did the old tie get to the cottage?
9   What did the police do to the man?
10 In what way is this story like *Aunt Suzie's Rooster?*

B *The writing skills*

1   Are there any parts of the story written as *scene* and not as *summary?*
2   What does the writer put in to get the reader to believe that the man could have behaved in the way the writer said in the story?
3   Are there any descriptive words and phrases used to make the dog seem like an evil person?
4   A *surprise ending* sometimes makes a story unconvincing (hard to believe) because it depends on some accidental happening or coincidence which is not likely to happen in real life. Does this story have a *surprise ending* depending on an accidental happening? If it does have a *surprise ending,* is it one that makes you doubt the story?
5   How much do you know about the man? Is he a *round character* in the story or a *flat character?*
6   What kind of atmosphere or mood does the writer manage to put into the story? Do you think you have an idea of how he did that?

C *The use of words*

1 Discuss which of the meanings below fits each of these words:

obscene (l.6)   *persistent* (l.33)   *villain* (l.38)   *ample* (l.76)
carnivorous (l.31)   *evaded* (l.31)   *incredible* (l.31)   *eradicate* (l.33)

a) dodged and avoided
b) cannot easily be believed
c) get rid of entirely
d) flesh-eating
e) guilty and wicked person
f) quite enough
g) indecent
h) keeping on trying and doing

2 Use each of these words in an oral sentence to describe an action, person or thing:

bolted (l.50)   *dangling* (l.68)   *darting* (l.69)   *sneaky* (l.108)
entrap (l.120)   *snarl* (l.127)

3 Which word in list A is related in form and meaning to another word in list B?

A   *irritating* (l.14)   *annoyance* (l.15)   *existed* (l.24)
    capable (l.52)   *invasion* (l.53)   *resolution* (l.63)
B   annoy   invade   irritable   existence   resolve   capacity,

Beaming out

Here are three ideas from which you might select one, if you wish, to work on this week, but you may have other ideas of your own. Put your story into your folder for discussion with your classmates.

1 Imagine being the black dog. Tell the story of yourself and the man, describing three or four scenes that took place, including, of course, the one in which the man shot at you.
2 Suppose that the police had to mount a hunt for the man who they thought had committed the murder. Narrate the story of the chase, giving the details of everything that happened.
3 Think of times you remember when one person provoked another, and the different ways in which it was done. Then in your imagination put two or three of them together in a story about two people, in which one of them does something very serious because of the other's provocation. Continue the story to a sad or happy end, but not by bringing in some surprise that has nothing to do with what went before.

20 BANJO
Denis Foster

Tuning in

In real life unpleasant and sad things happen, as well as happy ones. So, writers have to show us both kinds of experience. And we have to pay attention to both kinds, not only the pleasant ones—unless we wish to remain childish.

The writer of this story seems to have felt very strongly about Banjo, and felt he had to tell what happened to him. Perhaps he was being sentimental. Perhaps not.

(*obscurity* (1.1) = secrecy from the public; *resigned to* (1.24) = not trying to change; *macabre* (1.57) = having to do with death.)

B anjo lived and died in obscurity. Born on the street, he died on the street. Found in a garbage bin, his remains now rot in a garbage disposal dump.

He lived for three months, and in that time he made Helen and myself and a few others very happy, and caused no one any pain.

When I found Banjo, he was a weak and wiry little puppy, suspicious of all people, and very afraid of them. His ribs hung down in streaks from his back like banjo strings, and his head, which was all eyes, was ten times too big for his body. It rested precariously on his shoulders, and his ears perched on his head like floppy birds on a branch.

The first time I approached this little brown dog, he scrambled out of the overturned garbage bin, and stumbled, with his tail tucked between his bony legs, and his head turned warily in my direction, under the car whining. Every time I approached him, he would shift his position cleverly—moving from under one wheel to the other. I knew that he was afraid of me, but he also knew that I was afraid of him. He knew that I did not want to frighten or startle him in my effort to catch him. He knew, I think, that I did not want to chase him away. What he did not understand, was why.

And so he circled me, and I circled him from bumper to bumper. Eventually, after enticing him with a bowl of milk and stale bread, which he wisely refused, I gave up the chase and went upstairs to the kitchen resigned to the fact that I had been outwitted. Through the window I saw his spindly legs carry him bouncing down the drive and out into the street. Impulsively I ran downstairs after him. He had strolled into the next-door neighbour's yard and was nonchalantly smelling around behind the low entrance wall. I crept closer. He was

rustling in the grass behind the wall, occupied, not expecting me to
30 strike back, especially in somebody else's yard. I stepped softly,
slowly, crouching slightly behind the wall, with only my head
showing. Now we were opposite each other; he on one side of the
wall, I on the other. There he was backing me, completely unaware of
my presence. Then in a flash, my hands were down upon him. He
35 jumped and tried to wriggle out of my grasp, yelping, his head
waving madly, in utter disbelief and confusion.

In the living room of our house there was a large couch which was
pushed up against a wall. And it was here that Banjo spent his first
week with us. He was very much afraid of his new surroundings and
40 still very suspicious of our motives. He would sit behind the couch all
day without revealing himself, and every time we approached him he
would shiver all over like a vibrating banjo string.

At first Banjo would eat nothing. We tried bread soaked in milk,
and when he refused that, we tried milk and eggs; but he would have
45 none of it. He was so young and starved that we thought we should
wean him gradually on to harder food. However, after the first day of
trying in vain to get him to eat, we became desperate, thinking that he
would die at any moment. That night after dinner, however, our
worries came to an end. We had eaten ox-tail stew for dinner, and I put
50 the left over bones in a plate next to the couch, just as a last resort, not
thinking him old enough to eat such food. To my surprise, when

Banjo thought we were not looking he sneaked out from under the couch, and one by one the bones disappeared into his cave of solitude.

The next morning when I offered him some more bones, I held one in my hand and pushed it in front of Banjo's nose. He cocked his huge head to one side and eyed me inquiringly. He did not quite understand this macabre game. I wanted him out from behind the couch, he was aware of that much; but he was still too wary of human beings to realise that what I really wanted was to build up some sort of friendly relationship with him.

Hunger, however, makes a fool of man and dog alike, and eventually he took his first bone, shaking all over, from my hand.

From that moment our relationship developed. By the end of the first week he had ceased to live like a hermit and was walking, however unsteadily, around the house investigating every corner like a determined Sherlock Holmes.

The day soon came when Banjo followed us everywhere we went in the house.

Then the day of decision came. We opened the doors to Banjo for the first time since we had found him. He was free to stay or go. We watched him intently through the kitchen window as he sniffed his way slowly down the drive. He reached the gate, and there he sat down and contemplated the public road. He turned around, sat down again, and contemplated his surroundings. He looked back at the road outside, wagged his tail, and came pelting up the drive and into the house.

The last time I saw Banjo alive was around 7 o'clock one Sunday evening. We were watching television, and it was not until about one hour later that I really began to worry about him. I thought maybe he was next door.

I walked out into the front yard and whistled and called for him from the gate. But I did not hear the characteristic patter of his tiny feet. I walked out in the street. In the middle of the road lay a dark mass, a shadow.

I knew it was Banjo. I knew too that he was dead. I had never really expected to find him dead. Death was always something separate from life, something distant and fantastic. I bent down beside the body. His hind legs were spraddled out behind him and his body was bloated. There was a large gash along his stomach, not a puncture, but the skin had been ripped off and I saw the black tyre squeezing and pinching the flesh against the tar road. I saw the wheel turning over and the body being sucked under. The flattening lungs suddenly gasped. I felt the backbone and the ribs under the tyre, and the black rubber giving slightly as the bones snapped and splayed open and the guts squelched and burst inside the stretching skin. I heard the stifled cry that was drowned out by the drone of the motor. The front legs

151

forced upwards as the hind legs were crushed. The neck stretched and
the mouth gaped as the tongue rolled backwards into the throat. I saw
the wheel spin its full circle and the front legs and distorted head hit the
100 road. The shoulders bend under the head forcing the feet and head to
rest lengthways along the road. The slight gurgling noise in the throat
as the crushed intestines spit up brine on to the curled and bloody
tongue.

The body lay on the road cold and distorted.

105 A man on a bicycle rode slowly down the road singing a happy
indifferent tune to himself and the shadows of the night. I remember
standing on Mt Hillaby that morning listening to the church bells
ringing in some distant valley.

I removed the collar from around Banjo's neck and hopelessly
110 began to cry.

Talking about it

A *The events of the story*

1 Who or what was Banjo?
2 Why was he called Banjo?
3 How long did he live?
4 What was he doing when the narrator first saw him?
5 Where did he place himself when the narrator went towards him?
6 What did the narrator see from the kitchen window?
7 How was Banjo finally held?
8 Where did he take as his 'cave' in the house?
9 How did the family know that Banjo had decided to stay with
    them?
10 What happened to Banjo one Sunday evening?
11 Did the narrator see when it happened or did he just imagine
    seeing it happen?
12 Where was Banjo's body thrown?

B *The writing skills*

1 The end of the story is told at the very beginning. Does that spoil
   the story for you and make it uninteresting to read?
2 The story seems to have no theme or meaning that the writer
   wants you to think about. Would you agree that it has no theme? If
   you do, can you suggest why the author wrote it?
3 Do you think the story has a lot of sentimentality in it?
4 Some people might think the writer should not have used the
   word *macabre* (1.57) just for the narrator's game with the puppy.

They might think it is an exaggeration, and a bit of purple writing. Would you agree?

5   The first two paragraphs are written as *summary*, then the narration changes to the description of the *scene* or events actually taking place. Where else in the story do you also find a short bit of *summary?*

6   Do you see anything *ironic* about the man on a bicycle singing a happy tune?

7   *Characterisation* is how a writer shows you a person in action in a story, or explains about him or her. Is there any characterisation in this story?

8   We might say something is written in a *sensational* way when it is written just for the sake of exciting us, without being really necessary. Would you say the description of the death of the dog is *sensational* or not?

C   *Words to use*

1   In small groups of four or five, find each of these words in the story and get an idea of what each one might mean; then try to use each one in an oral sentence of your own. Use as many as you can.

warily (l.14)   *whining* (l.15)   *startle* (l.18)   *impulsively* (l.26)
nonchalantly (l.27)   *unaware* (l.33)   *wriggle* (l.35)   *yelping* (l.35)
vibrating (l.42)   *sneaked* (l.52)   *wary* (l.58)   *sniffed* (l.71)
spraddled (l.88)   *bloated* (l.89)   *gash* (l.89)   *squelched* (l.95)
gaped (l.98)   *distorted* (l.99)   *gurgling* (l.101)

2   Discuss which one of the words below each sentence best fits into the blank space in the sentence.

a)   He sat and _____ what he should do.
     existed   contemplated   bolted   snarled

b)   I could not understand their _____ for doing that.
     motives   annoyance   capacity   invasion

c)   She is very _____ of anyone who comes to the gate.
     irritable   capable   ample   suspicious

d)   Do you want to live all by yourself like a _____ ?
     resort   brine   hermit   characteristic

e)   The thieves _____ the police and got away.
     occupied   outwitted   determined   sneaked

f)   The rock was balancing _____ on the edge of the cliff above us.
     inquiringly   eventually   precariously   hopelessly

153

g) I was so _____ that I would have done anything at all.
   desperate   perched   wary   stale
h) They were _____ him to eat by offering him meat.
   rustling   crouching   investigating   enticing
i) She preferred to live in _____ rather than mix with those people.
   relationship   surroundings   solitude   disbelief
j) The visitor was looking very _____ at the picture on the wall.
   intently   spindly   cleverly   impulsively

Beaming out

Perhaps you might like to use one of these or some other idea this week to add to your collection in your folder.

1 If you have ever suffered the loss of a pet make up a story about it so that a reader can share your experience with it and your feelings.
2 Suppose Banjo had grown up into a faithful guard-dog. Make up a story of how he saved the family one day from some serious danger.